New Glory

GÜNTER DE BRUYN

NEW GLORY

A NOVEL

Translated from the German
by David Burnett

NORTHWESTERN UNIVERSITY PRESS

EVANSTON, ILLINOIS

Northwestern University Press
www.nupress.northwestern.edu

Published 2009 by Northwestern University Press. Originally published as *Neue Herrlichkeit*, copyright © 1984 Mitteldeutscher Verlag, Halle (Saale). All rights reserved S. Fischer Verlag GmbH, Frankfurt am Main.

Printed in the United States of America

10 9 8 7 6 5 4 3 2 1

Library of Congress Cataloging-in-Publication Data

De Bruyn, Günter, 1926–
    [Neue Herrlichkeit. English]
    New glory : a novel / Günter de Bruyn ; translated from the German by David Burnett.
        p. cm.
    ISBN 978-0-8101-2552-0 (pbk. : alk. paper)
    1. Germany (East)—Social conditions—Fiction. I. Burnett, David L. (David Laurence), 1973– II. Title.
    PT2662.R88N4813 2009
    833.914—dc22

                                            2009027747

♾ The paper used in this publication meets the minimum requirements of the American National Standard for Information Sciences—Permanence of Paper for Printed Library Materials, ANSI Z39.48-1992.

CONTENTS

ONE BIG FAMILY

Before Viktor himself is introduced, our readers will get to hear what others have to say about him. Olga says he has a naturalness about him, but doesn't get a chance to expand on the meaning of this ambiguous term since Max—who can never resist the urge to contradict her but in this case doesn't have anything contradictory to say, because he, too, only knows Viktor from hearsay—says in at least a *tone* of contradiction, "Let's just wait and see," to which Olga replies, "At least he's not conceited."

They say this at the kitchen table, a few hours before Viktor arrives. Here in the kitchen they can speak their minds, because guests aren't allowed to enter at lunchtime. It's an unwritten law that everyone knows, and newcomers who don't know never barge in more than once, being frightened off by the icy stares that greet them.

The nine people gathered at the table could easily be taken for one big family, and since they live together and eat together, they *are* in a certain sense one big family, though not related, or only partly so—a family made up of fragments of several families. Related to each other are, first of all, Tita and Thilde; second, Max and Püppi; and third, Olga, Püppi, Gabi, Thomas, and Manuela. Only one of them is unrelated to the rest: Sebastian, the gardener, who lets the hair on his head and face grow as it pleases, although it bothers him occasionally, when eating tomato soup, for instance, which leaves traces of red on the whiskers around his mouth.

At the head of the table sits Max, the boss, who later comes up with something derogatory about Viktor after all: he's the kind of person that makes demands. Twice Viktor's mother has requested by phone that her son receive a quiet room. That's twice too often for Max. "He'll probably ask me to tie the cows' mouths shut so he can have his peace and quiet to write," says Max, while trying to feed Püppi, who's sitting on his knee.

Püppi rarely feels like eating, and when Max coaxes her with "Another spoon for Papa!" she presses her lips together and swats at the spoon. It's Gabi who has to wipe up the mess, while Max just laughs at his comical little girl. He looks around invitingly with his sky-blue eyes but doesn't find anyone to laugh along with him.

Meat, considered by Max to be the foundation of child nutrition, is especially repulsive to Püppi. Only when he prechews it for her and spits it back onto the spoon will she eat it, without displaying the slightest relish. Then again, she never displays anything of the sort; at best she is calm and content. Her bawling, however, is loud and fierce and sets in whenever Max takes more than three steps away from her. Püppi is daddy's girl in every respect. Only when she's sleeping can he be seen without her. Max is proud of her attachment, which presumably is more a need for protection. Olga, her mother, has little time for her, whereas Gabi and Thomas take every available opportunity to harass her. No sooner does Max look the other way than Gabi pulls out one of her curly blond hairs or Thomas threatens to poke her with a needle. Though capable of letting out a piercing scream, three-year-old Püppi hasn't learned how to talk yet. Olga says it's because she's pampered and lazy. When Thilde suggests to Max that he take his little girl to the doctor, he responds, "Why should she talk if she doesn't want to? I understand her well enough."

To the right and left of Max, at the first seats on the long side of the table, sit Gabi and Thomas. They're twins but don't look it, which every now and then causes Max to wonder if they sprang from the same father. Not seldom does he remark facetiously that one person alone would have trouble being that cheeky. But his comment is inappropriate, because Gabi is never cheeky. On the contrary, she's always trying to curry favor—with nothing to show for it. She always volunteers to do the dirty work, and Max just assumes she enjoys it, rendering a thank-you unnecessary. Olga never bothers to praise Gabi's industriousness either. Admittedly, the pudgy girl is hard to grow fond of. She's silly and slovenly. When Sebastian, the gardener, strokes her hair out of pity, she snuggles up to him and acts like a baby, embarrassing him and stifling his good intentions. Unlike her brother, she's unable to hide her ignorance in school and has flunked sixth grade as a consequence.

Thomas, on the other hand, has learned to be nimble-minded in his running battle with Max—for the sake of survival, you might say after hearing Max talk about him. He says he's afraid of wringing the boy's neck someday—when Thomas pours water into the gas tank of his car, for example, or saws into the rungs of the ladder in the hayloft. "That dirty rascal is gonna do me in," he says, when the schnapps brings tears of self-pity to his eyes.

Thomas admits that he intends to do just that. He boasts about the cruelty of his imagination and takes pleasure in fantasizing about accidents in which Max dies an excruciating death. He shows off what a cool smoker he is while delving into the gory details. Supposedly the cigarettes he likes best are not the ones from the store but the ones he steals from Max's pocket. Max caught him only once. Thomas proudly displays the scars on his back. You'll never see a tear on his freckled face.

His tablemate is the bearded Sebastian, who tries in vain at every meal to strike up a conversation with Manuela, sitting across from him. Unlike her half-sister Püppi, she knows how to talk; she simply chooses not to when she's in the kitchen. She gets along just fine by nodding or shaking her head and promptly dismisses her detractors with a "Phh!" Whether she's as pretty as Olga claims is hard to tell, her face being hidden behind a heavy layer of pancake makeup. She likes to show off her figure though, in tight-fitting pants and blouses, and appreciative comments occasionally prompt an airy smile. That she plans to become a stewardess with *Interflug* when she graduates from school in the summer isn't news to anyone, what with Olga always bringing it up. "She'll end up walking the streets!" is what Max has to say about her. He points out the young men from Görtz, Prötz, and

Schwedenow who circle the house on their rattling mopeds whenever Manuela is grounded.

"I raise my daughter just as strict as I was raised," Olga says, sitting furthest away from Max at the far end of the table, to the left. "I'm every bit as strict a mother as my own mother was to me."

Everything Olga says ends up being long-winded due to a tendency to repeat herself, particularly when she's loaded with alcohol, which is often enough but sometimes goes unnoticed. She's a closet drinker and knows how to control herself even in the most severe state of intoxication. In fact, she's so good at it, you wonder what she gets out of drinking in the first place if she can never let go of her inhibitions. Of course, her coworkers (though not the guests) are well aware of her drinking habits, and she knows that they know. Still, she never lets go of her inner brakes. If she can't walk without staggering, she'll simply stay put, and if her tongue shows signs of paralysis, she's quite capable of keeping quiet. She's a heavy smoker and is constantly lighting up. It's surprising how well her slender frame tolerates it all. She's well preserved, despite being a mother of four. The only thing about her that really looks old are her lips, which are little more than lines.

Max and Olga aren't married. Her name is Frau Kranz and his is Herr Brüggemann. They're living in sin, as folks in the village say. "Get married?" says Max, "With her and her brood? I'd rather put a noose around my neck!"

He doesn't say that at the table of course. If his temper isn't flaring, he knows how to behave himself—for the sake of Tita and Thilde, sitting to the right and left of Olga, Tita next to Sebastian, Thilde on the opposite side.

The name Tita basically means "grandma." Thilde came up with it once as a child, nobody knows why anymore. Everyone here calls her that, and *only* that. Some of them don't even know that her real name is Frau Lüderitz. Tita is eighty-four. She was the one giving the orders around here before Max came. And her authority is still unchallenged. The punctuality here is thanks to her. One glance of hers at the kitchen clock fills dawdlers with dread and makes them want to apologize. Max wouldn't dare make any changes to the buildings without first asking her permission. He solicits her advice on other matters, too, though often gets only gibberish for an answer because she rarely understands what he's saying. She's hard of hearing. But you can't be sure of that either. In purely legal terms, house and home still belong to her. She's spent almost her whole life here. Her granddaughter, Thilde, too.

It is the day of Viktor's arrival, and Thilde still doesn't know which room to make up. Max planned on the gable room. The typewriter noises at night would bother only Tita, and she can't hear anyway.

Son of the Father

At about the same time, Viktor has just said his first good-bye to his mother (in the apartment). The second one (outside) is yet to come. He would have liked to prevent it but couldn't muster up the courage. His mother had to miss work in order to see him off—in other words, she's making a sacrifice. He therefore owes her a bit of ceremony.

The elevator carries them down from the thirteenth floor. Viktor is looking at the floor indicator above the door, which is only proper in an elevator. His mother, however, is looking at her son: a little enamored, a little concerned, and not without a hint of scorn. Viktor is familiar with the look in her eyes and knows how to interpret it. Only her being enamored and concerned is genuine. The scornfulness is artificial and serves to signal detachment. Although a modern woman, the way she sees it, is entitled to feelings and allowed to show them, she has to prove that she can keep them under control. Thus, her tears are invariably accompanied by a witty remark, her depressions expertly explained, and when she endeavors to lend her outward appearance a semblance of youthfulness, a comment about the vanity of older women is sure to follow.

Just as Viktor feared, Agnola (that's her name, and that's exactly what she has Viktor call her) links arms with him on the street. She's smaller than him and wears her hair short, and since her exuberance is, to her, an obvious indication that she's still young at heart, she fancies that everyone takes mother and son for sister and brother. Her admirers are eager to confirm it, but Viktor suspects she drops them hints beforehand. She needs the appreciation of others and can provoke it if she has to. Her son, too, has been trained to serve her in this capacity. His task, particularly in the company of others, is to bolster the community of Agnola admirers. More difficult than the task itself, however, is believing that his mother is really so naïve. Does she not realize that the respect she enjoys is not thanks to her beauty and charm but to the fact that she was married to Kösling?

Viktor can't help being skeptical about Agnola's naïvety. He himself has always had problems being a Kösling, ever since childhood. He has never been able to decide if having a big shot for a father is a blessing or a curse. It makes his life easier in some respects, but complicates it too—for instance, in that people are always ascribing to him motivations he doesn't have. His father is praised as a role model so friends and colleagues assume he's one for Viktor, too. They forget that only someone high enough up and far enough away is suitable as such. And how are they to know that Viktor is unambitious? He keeps it a secret, having learned his lesson from negative experience with his mother and father. He has no desire to rise above others, commanding over and directing them; he's happy to just get along with them.

This has always caused him problems—problems invariably linked to his father, causally or otherwise. For he keeps on having to ask himself if people know whose son he is, and if they do, if it's because of or despite his father that they're nasty or nice to him. The problem is not that Viktor's father casts an obscuring shadow over him; it's knowing whether the shadow will afford him protection or not.

Of course the difficulties multiply as soon as he finds himself in unfamiliar circles—admittedly, seldom enough—and among people who, when he mentions his name, inevitably ask him, "Kösling? What do you mean Kösling?" without supposing there could be a relation. If he explains how he got the name, it's considered boasting, whereas if he keeps it a secret, it's construed as shiftiness.

As long as he took the view (following not his inclinations but conventional notions about being young) that life is an adventure, and that surviving it is all the more admirable the more you suffer inwardly, he could persuade himself that he enjoyed being around

9

people who didn't suspect his family ties and only judged him by his words and deeds. But sometimes all they did was ignore him. Thus, he was quick to discern that needlessly exposing yourself to situations you can't measure up to is acting contrary to reason. That's why he prefers to be on familiar ground, where people know who he is and where he can rely on amiability to counter the danger of not being respected for what he is.

And that's the reason he immediately agreed to his mother's suggestion that the working vacation granted to him by the Foreign Ministry should be spent at the Friedrich Schulze-Decker Home. Because the establishment, however old and creaky, belongs to the Ministry, and therefore offers him a guarantee that they know who they're dealing with by taking him in. Of course his mother had other reasons to opt for this out of the many possibilities available to her son. She wants him to finish his dissertation (the whole purpose of the vacation) and is eager to shield him from potential distractions. The home is located in a remote area that is all the more sleepy in wintertime. The small towns nearby, which are hard to reach without a car, offer a movie theater at best, and the regional capital is far away. The home is nearly deserted this time of year because few people, mostly elderly, are willing to put up with a lack of amenities for the sake of peace and quiet. Hence the allures of society will hardly tempt him to flee his desk.

The litany of exhortations so familiar to Viktor is repeated during the brief walk from apartment to parking lot. The driver shows that he knows who he's driving. He gets out of the car, opens the door, and says a friendly word or two about the luggage already stowed in the trunk. Although he's the only spectator, his presence encourages Agnola to put on a powerful display of motherliness. The hugs and kisses, the warnings and jovial threats cease only when Viktor frees himself from her clasp and gets into the vehicle. Agnola stays behind in a pose meant to express melancholy.

Once he's done waving, Viktor heaves a sigh of relief intended for the driver. As expected, it's greeted with a chuckle, followed—just to play it safe—by a comment about the remarkable youthfulness of Frau Kösling. Viktor, however, doesn't feel like talking about his mother. He asks about their destination. The driver says it's a dreary place, located, pardon his saying so, in the ass crack of the world. Agnola described it as austere and Prussian and was hoping it would stimulate her son's work, which has to do with Prussia. Viktor's path in life has culminated in a diplomatic career, but also included a degree in history, which is still weighing down on him in the form of a long overdue dissertation. "The Foreign Policy of the Prussian Government during the French Revolution with Particular Emphasis on the Effects of Artisan and Peasant Unrest in the Provinces" is its topic, and Viktor doesn't know much more than that just yet. But it's all in the books, he just has to read them. He has it all planned. Through strict discipline in rural isolation he intends to catch up in a matter of weeks on what he's been neglecting for years. So inspired was he by the thought of an ascetic work routine, interrupted only by meals and lonely walks full of creative thoughts, that it was he and not his mother who suggested leaving the car, a potential means of fleeing, at home. This is why he's traveling in an official vehicle, one from the Ministry, which apart from himself and his chauffeur is conveying two suitcases full of clothes, a typewriter, and numerous boxes of books.

They leave Berlin and head east on the autobahn, eventually exiting to the south. After passing through several towns, the driver announces their imminent arrival. The bumpy road, widened by a footpath, is flanked by apple trees. Barren fields stretch to the right and left. Then the pinewood begins. There where a sandy path crosses the road and signs point the way to Prötz and Schwedenow, the marshy fringes of a lake extend to the road. Small patches of reeds and rushes grow here and there under trees. At the edge of the woods, the driver points to the left: in the middle of the field, about a kilometer away, a group of redbrick buildings heaves into sight on the horizon, their windowless and doorless backs turned dismissively to the road.

Just before Görtz there is a curve in the road. A dirt road branches off behind it which, as the driver explains, is known as Dead Man's Road because it leads to the cemetery in Prötz, where the Görtzer, too, are buried. Plum trees grow along the waysides. Deep ruts in the road make for a hazardous drive. Shards of glass and old mattresses are dodged along the way; the road to the cemetery seems to lead to the dump as well. Twisting and turning, it winds its way uphill. Only when they get there does it become clear what the redbrick buildings are: a farmstead. Barns and cowsheds are built around the farmyard on three sides. The house, two-storied, is on the fourth, its handsome facade, with round-arched windows and rosette ornaments, facing the road. "Built in 1895," reads the inscription above the door. Another inscription is visible on the glazed-tile roof, yellow letters against a crimson background: NEW GLORY.

The gate to the left of the house is open, and the car pulls into the farmyard. Max, who's standing there ready to greet them with Püppi on his arm, opens the car door. "Welcome, Comrade Kösling," he says. "Good thing you made it. We're in for nasty weather."

THILDE, STILL FACELESS

Before Viktor even sets foot on the grounds of New Glory, a brilliant display of what Olga will later call his good-heartedness has occasion to unfold.

Still sitting in the car, he hands boxes out to Max and explains why they're so heavy: full of books, he needs them for his work, which is the reason he's here—to write his dissertation. He's virtually forgotten how to write by hand; he needs the typewriter, which, unfortunately, makes a little noise. That's why he'd again like to request a secluded room—he doesn't want to bother anyone.

"That won't be a problem, Comrade Kösling," says Max, who takes two boxes under his arms and two in his hands and heads for the house, from which Tita emerges in coat and kerchief. She approaches the car with hurried steps, raps the metal body with her cane, saying, "It's about time you came!" then thrusts herself into the vehicle.

Tita is an imposing figure: large and stout without being fat. Solidly built, as she likes to put it. She groans while climbing in, has a hard time finding a place for her walking stick, and, once she's seated, expresses relief: "So!" Her face is lined with wrinkles and dominated by her chin, which is too pointed and too long, with an occasional facial hair growing on it, eight or ten of them perhaps. She looks at Viktor with her beady, gray-green eyes and, sternly but in good spirits, proclaims, "We can be on our way now!"

Viktor looks around for help, but there's none to be had; the driver, too, has gone into the house (with the luggage from the trunk).

Püppi, who is left behind in the yard, plops down on the concrete and starts to scream. Tita slams the car door shut.

"Pardon me," says Viktor, "but I don't think this is where you belong."

"Where to, where to!" replies Tita, in a tone as though she were mocking someone. "Where to, then? To Klein-Kietz, of course."

Although Viktor has never had to deal with the hard of hearing before, he quickly grasps the situation. He shouts his sentence one more time in Tita's ear, and when he thinks he spots something like a spark of recognition on her face, adds that this is not a taxi but an official car, to which Tita responds, "What of it!" and puts on a pouty face.

Viktor looks helpless, and that's exactly what he is: a state he often finds himself in (the reason why this little episode, which will be over before long, is being recounted here in the first place). He has no idea who Tita is or where Klein-Kietz is located. What he does know is that he is no match for strong-minded people, young or old. Because they always have aims they try to assert, and since his own aims amount to nothing more than the desire to coexist peacefully with others, he's ultimately forced to acquiesce. He can't bear it when people are angry with him.

He finally yells in Tita's ear that he'll see what can be done, thereby achieving the desired effect. She says, somewhat mollified, "What must be, must be." She even smiles, and for Viktor the world is put to rights again, if only briefly. For when he asks his chauffeur to take the old lady back home to her village located God knows where, he naturally encounters his wrath—on account of the weather forecast, calling for high winds, cold, freezing rain and snow. The driver remains silent, but his facial expression says it all. Viktor does his best to appease him—it can't be far, she doesn't even have any luggage— but it is Thilde's intervention that frees him of his worries this time. She opens the car door and says, not loudly but articulately, "Come on, Tita, this is not where you belong!"

The fact that, by sheer coincidence, Thilde uses virtually the same words as Viktor will, of course, be accorded a deeper significance later on. For now Viktor notices other things: first, that Thilde can't properly pronounce an *s* (because she lisps); second, that her altogether adult voice forms a stark contrast to her wispy, childlike frame, which he can see from knee to shoulder in the open car door; and, finally, that *her* words are more successful than his. Because in no time flat Tita cries out, "Criminy!" and clambers out of the car. Thilde takes her by the arm and escorts her back to the house. Viktor glimpses the two of them from behind. He tries to picture the face that has so far eluded his gaze. He's good at that kind of thing.

A Permanent Guest

Agnola was right—the home is virtually empty. Apart from Viktor, only two other guests are lodging there at present. Viktor meets them on the tour Max gives him.

On the upper floor of the side building to the left—which used to be stables and now houses the kitchen and dining room—adjacent to Max and Olga's rooms, lives Herr Köpke, a rotund bald-headed man who always wears green when he's on vacation. Viktor thinks he has seen him before at the Ministry but has never actually worked with him. Herr Köpke, Viktor soon learns, spends his vacation at the home each year without his family. He always comes in the wintertime, when things slow down, and never during school breaks, when his children might be inclined to follow him. "If there's any point in vacation, it's got to be a vacation from the family," he explains, "because family is more exhausting than work." Herr Köpke is a hunter. For years he has been a member of the Görtz hunting collective without ever taking part in any of their drives, battues, or shooting parties, since hunting only appeals to him when he can do it on his own. At dawn or at dusk, all alone in the blind—nothing beats that as far as he's concerned. When he isn't eating, sleeping, or hunting, he's invariably watching TV, for that, too, says Herr Köpke, provides a measure of seclusion. Viktor, with a bewildered smile, though not without respect, shows his sympathy for Herr Köpke's vacationing idiosyncrasies by suppressing his questions about bucks and deer and leaving the nimrod in peace.

The former barn, across from the house, serves as a garage and workshop. Two and a half cars can be seen there between dismounted engines and pieces of bodywork. One of them belongs to Max, the other one and a half as well, although only temporarily. They were wrecked by friends, and Max, dumb as he is, decided to buy them for way too much money. The losses will be enormous if he ever repairs and resells them, not even counting the labor. Max, scrunching his face as if in pain, claims that they are always taking advantage of his good-naturedness, the scoundrels (he doesn't call them by name). Even the cows, in the stall to the right under the hayloft, cause him grief. Everybody wants his milk, the real, creamy, yellow kind you can't buy in stores, yet no one is willing to lend him a hand.

Viktor can't make any promises either, though he does express his appreciation for the fact that it certainly must be hard work. He also praises the smell of the barn and, later in the farmyard, the animal warmth, which he calls homey. "What a healthy place to grow up!" he says to Püppi, who accompanies the men nestled in her father's arm. The child ignores Viktor's remark; her papa, however, is beaming. Viktor, it seems, has found the way to Max's heart.

They hurry back to the house through an icy gale and drizzle. The ground floor is divided down the middle by a hallway. Tita and Thilde's rooms face toward Prötz; the office and recreation room, where the telephone and TV can be found, are located on the other side facing Görtz. Upstairs, just under the roof, lives Sebastian, the gardener. One floor down are the guest rooms, which except for two are vacant. Viktor is staying in one of the gable rooms at the end of the hall, right above Tita. The room closest to the stairs belongs to Frau Erika, who is standing in the doorway waiting to receive them and is introduced by Max as "our permanent guest."

Frau Erika has met the new guest before, in former days. He was probably three or four years old when she saw him last, back when her husband was still alive and Jan (Viktor's father) was still married to Agnola. What a cute little fellow Viktor was back then, and now he's all grown up, so strapping and handsome, with a mustache that's quite becoming; he's just a little green around the gills, that's all, thin and pale like a prince, Prince Hamlet perhaps. My oh my, how time

17

flies! It's all you can do to keep up with your age, she says, laughing, since she knows how young she still looks with her meticulous bleach-blond hair, never mind that it's thinning a little.

She pulls the young man into her room with both hands. He and Max are obliged to take a seat. She offers them milk (which Max refuses) and cookies from a crystal candy dish. "Now, tell me," she says to Viktor, "how you've been all these years and what poor Agnola is up to and if she's still so beautiful." But she doesn't give Viktor a chance to tell her. Her own urge to communicate carries her away, and she does all the talking herself, so that after two glasses of milk Viktor knows everything he needs to know about her.

Everyone here just calls her Frau Erika, at her own request. Her long surname, she feels, doesn't do her justice as an individual. When people hear the name Schulze-Decker, they think of the antifascist hero and later minister after whom the rest home was named; they don't think of her, the minister's wife. She doesn't want to adorn herself with borrowed plumes, which is why she seldom mentions her husband in the talks she gives, a fact that Max considers scandalous; after all, she lives off the hero's pension, which Olga calls sizable and Max calls gigantic. He draws his conclusions from the size of the tips she gives the children for fetching her linseed oil and yeast from the village store, and from the exorbitant price she pays him for the milk, every day, of her own volition. When Max puts on a token display of protest, she invariably makes a depreciatory remark about money being a worldly good.

The yeast she eats with nothing added, the linseed oil with cottage cheese she makes herself. She shows off the equipment (jugs, cheesecloth, and a hot plate) to Viktor, who's extremely interested. Frau Erika needs no more sustenance than this. Her body would become clogged if she ate anything more; this way it stays supple inside. She's given up the tobacco she was once addicted to. The only poison she can't do without is coffee. Every two or three hours she brews herself a pot. Helgalein keeps her supplied, bringing it from Berlin when she visits her older sister each weekend. Helgalein also takes care of the spacious Berlin apartment, which Frau Erika uses as overnight accommodation when national holidays demand her presence in the capital. On such occasions she makes herself visible with enthusiastic waving from her spot up on the platform, because she knows that the inhabitants of Görtz, Prötz, and New Glory are sitting in front of their television screens trying to see if they can spot her. She's never inclined to stay in Berlin for very long though; the people there have no time for each other.

Her home is the rest home. Here she's in touch with nature, humans, and animals. Her room was furnished by Helgalein in exact accordance with her needs and tastes. The refrigerator, coffee machine, and hot plate are hidden behind a curtain. Next to the sofa bed is a record player, from which the muffled sounds of operetta melodies can be heard. A shelf is filled with dolls from around the world, souvenirs from when she used to accompany her husband on his travels. The electric heater that looks like a fireplace is also from abroad. When you turn it on, flickering logs give off a surprisingly realistic glow. The walls are adorned with photos, all of them displaying a younger Erika in varied apparel and costume. She was an actress before she became a minister's wife and can give a detailed account of every one of her former roles for an admiring Viktor. What she can't remember are the lines; she forgot them all as fast as she learned them. "The essence of life, my prince," she says, "is its transitoriness, which, viewed from a different angle, is nothing but its intransitoriness."

Frau Erika isn't sick but not exactly healthy either. You might say she's afflicted—with cold feet, cold hands, palpitations, headaches, and insomnia. When she lies awake at night, she contemplates the soul, which is what she means by intransitoriness. Souls don't die, they simply change location. When our body is gone, as Frau Erika puts it, the soul migrates to another body, a newly born one, be it human or animal. Relocation takes place according to merit. For example, the soul of a person who beats his cows when he's angry, like Max does, can expect no better a dwelling the next time around than the body of, say, a wood louse. Granted, Frau Erika doesn't know exactly where her soul was before, but she does have dim recollections of a former life. Anyone can have insights like these, even more lucid ones than hers, if only they are able to gaze deeply enough into their souls. That's something that can be learned, she's sure of that. All you need is patience.

Püppi hardly has the patience to listen to Frau Erika, and she lets Max know it by clamoring to go. Viktor indicates the same, although somewhat more politely: he has to unpack, settle in, then get to work straightaway, because he's only got ten weeks. But he promises in leaving that during his breaks he, too, will plumb the depths of his soul and explore its prehistory. Frau Erika is pleased.

Alone in his room, he actually does try being introspective but to no avail. He closes his eyes so as to focus solely on his inner self yet only manages to see himself from the outside: the way he sits there gloomily, leaning on the tiled stove in a cramped and run-down room, where he'll be banished for months, joyless and all by his lonesome; and the way he listens to the storm outside that, despite the windows being closed, stirs the curtains and sends a chilly breath of air all the way to his belly, while his rear end pressed against the tiles seems hot to the point of glowing. To be sure, he has recollections aplenty, but not the kind Frau Erika had in mind; his have to do with the apartment in Berlin, with food, company, hot drinks, warm baths, and toasty rooms.

He doesn't expect to hold out here for long. The still unpacked boxes and suitcases encourage the thought of fleeing. But asking Max for a ride back would be too humiliating. He'll have to hike to the neighboring village and call for a taxi from there. His luggage can always be sent for later.

He slips on his coat, sneaks downstairs, and leaves the house. With rapid strides he takes a left and heads downhill toward the woods, behind which Prötz is said to be located. The wind propels him from behind. The dismal January day is coming to an end, colder than it began. Although it's raining still in tiny droplets, the grass is stiffened with frost. Below the pines the cemetery begins. Viktor wends his way between the graves toward where he assumes the village will be but doesn't make it very far. A ravine (which he later learns is called May Valley) blocks his path: the ravine, to wit, is full of trash. It's gotten dark in the meantime, and the woods around him are rustling, creaking, and groaning eerily. He decides to give up his escape plans and turn back. Struggling against the freezing wind, he's happy to find the path again.

Someone is calling his name when he reaches the house: there's a phone call for him. He recognizes Thilde's voice, rushes into the office on the left, and leaves the door open to see Thilde walk by. She does pass by, but closes the door from the hall outside, making herself all but invisible. Viktor puts the receiver to his ear and says, "Hello, Agnola!"

Son of the Mother

Until Olga rings the dinner bell, mother and son have time for a chat. It's become a habit for them to do so almost every evening, and the physical distance between them is no reason to break with tradition. His mother is still in her office, where she makes and maintains worldwide contacts to family planning associations. She won't be leaving soon; the icy roads make it dangerous to drive, and traveling from Berlin to Potsdam by train seems too adventurous to her. She'll work late and spend the night at Viktor's apartment instead. She asks him for permission, jokingly.

Viktor is wary of talking about people at the home without knowing how soundproof the walls are, so his mother does most of the talking. She's never at a loss for words, especially when she has news about his father, like she does now. In that respect, their conversation is like every other one between mother and son: it revolves around Viktor's father (whom she refers to as J.K.). It was that way before the divorce and hasn't changed since. For all her efforts to detach herself from Viktor's father emotionally, she's invariably forced to keep an eye on him so as to gauge the gap—hopefully widening—between them. So often does she tell herself that her life is more peaceful, comfortable, even more pleasant without him that she's finally come to believe it. What gnaws at her is nothing but envy: she begrudges him his younger wife. But, thanks to her son, she's one up on her. It's only for his sake, so she claims, that she keeps in touch with J.K. at all, however seldom. It's also on account of Viktor that she tends to idealize J.K., who is supposed to serve as a role model. Because only her son's success can prove what a loss she's been to his father.

She's blind to the fact that her ambition for Viktor prevents him from developing any of his own; and Viktor, for his part, has no intention of undeceiving her. That could become a source of conflict—a conflict he hasn't learned to deal with. He's used to being the person people want him to be. When his father was around, everything conformed to him, the almighty—to his work, his habits, opinions, and whims. Viktor, the child, learned early on that "good" meant what pleased his father, and "bad" was what his father disliked.

On the phone with his mother, Viktor is now told that J.K. is ill, news that strikes him as both alarming and amusing. The man who was always brimming with strength, who once thought weakness defeatist and sickness morally offensive—a man of this sort is hard to picture as a patient. The lion suddenly feels like a worm; the demigod who had no need for doctors and priests has now discovered that he, too, is mortal; his formidable power is now matched by his misery. He feels not only smitten by fate but scorned by it as well, because of all things it's his prostate that's ailing him. In his circles, one goes down honorably with a heart attack, but not like this. A giant who howls in pain when his urine won't flow is not a man anymore but a clown. He says this on the phone to his ex-wife after leaving the specialist clinic (which, incidentally, is located not far from New Glory). He can yammer all he wants to her but is ashamed to admit his weaknesses to his new wife.

When Viktor's mother, reporting on his sick father, says, "So I'm good enough to listen and commiserate," it's supposed to sound spiteful but ends up sounding proud. She wants Viktor to know how much she still means to his father. That strengthens the bond between father and son, she says. For the very same reason, his father is repeatedly told how strong the tie is between mother and son. That's why his father feels obliged to ask about him all the time, Viktor assumes. This time J.K. was interested in the progress being made on his son's dissertation. After all, honorary doctorates aside, Viktor's father never did manage to get a doctorate himself, as Agnola is quick to point out.

Viktor now gets a chance to demonstrate that the only thing on his mind is his dissertation. His mother hears about his elaborate pre-planning, which he'll be starting right away—after dinner, that is. He's going to make a kind of calendar, with two columns for every day for the next ten weeks. The first column will indicate the planned number of written pages, the second column the actual number. He'll take stock at the end of each week so as to keep track of whether he's ahead of or behind schedule. When he's finished with the planning calendar, he'll draw up an outline of his dissertation—first a rough draft, then a more detailed version, complete with decimal numbers. Each subheading will receive a separate sheet, which he'll file in binders so that every new thought he has in the course of his work or during his walks can be promptly and properly placed.

"It's snowing here," Agnola remarks, happy that she didn't hazard the drive to Potsdam.

Viktor looks out the window, but since the night is black he sees nothing but his reflection in the glass. He likes how he looks, casually seated at his desk with the receiver to his ear, and holds the pose for a while longer even after his mother hangs up. He heard the door open across the hall and hopes that Thilde will enter his room. But the footfalls retreat down the hall and make for the yard. So he, too, heads down the hall toward the yard, through cold and wind to the dining hall, where the table is already set and there's no one to be seen but the lonesome hunter, Köpke. He invites Viktor to watch TV with him after supper, but Viktor declines. Duty is calling. It's time to hit the books.

Getting to Work

Viktor has barely returned to his spot at the stove when it dawns on him that his planning for this evening is unrealistic. He's forgotten the preparatory work: unpacking his clothes and books and arranging his papers.

What he calls his papers are actually scraps of paper of every imaginable size containing notes he's made throughout the course of three not entirely unproductive years: bibliographic references, thought fragments, quotes from the classics, things like that. These he keeps in four folders, in utter disarray, as he's long since lost track of what the numbers mean that grace them. He also collects newspaper clippings. These have little to do with his actual topic but are intended to shed light on related subjects, which have meanwhile slipped his mind. He likes to clip out articles to give himself the feeling that his newspaper reading wasn't entirely pointless.

Viktor opens up the newspaper each and every day, just like his parents do. It's an acquired habit, like washing himself or brushing his teeth: a compulsion that, through sufficient repetition, has become self-perpetuating. His daily paper reading doesn't take up too much of his time though. Practice has cut down his reading time from year to year, and his eyes are trained to find with only a fleeting glance the words that really matter: his name, for instance (which never, of course, refers to him but to J.K.), the name of his highest-ranking superior, the name of his ministry, and, more recently, the names of the countries he's specializing in: Austria, Italy, Liechtenstein, and Switzerland. Even if he counts only his regular compulsory reading (leaving aside the other, mostly foreign, papers he often has to peruse), he can easily claim to have leafed through more newspaper pages in his lifetime than book pages.

This is what he often tells himself, apologetically, when he struggles to read books. Their dead, evenly printed pages stifle his energy and discourage him. Each page looks just like the next; he desperately hunts for pictures, is grateful for every bit of italics or boldfaced type, and skims ahead in the hope that a new chapter will soon arrive and offer some diversion. He wishes that all books were the way some textbooks are: the important things framed to attract attention, the irrelevant rest—the fine print—unmasked as superfluous. He has come to appreciate library books showing signs of use from industrious students. He rapidly makes sense of each individual system of markings, can soon tell if the blue checks, the red underlining, or the black dots are more valuable, and gleefully glides from climax to climax in the footsteps of his anonymous predecessors. If he's lucky, he can even decipher and absorb the notes in the margins.

He has no problem unpacking his clothes, neatly piles his underwear, shirts, and sweaters in the spacious wardrobe, and has a shelf left over for his shaving gear and cosmetics, the little shelf above the sink not being big enough for him. He has a look at himself in the mirror, combs his hair, and wonders where there's a hairdresser in the area. He then takes his place by the stove again and ponders where to put his books. The shelf on the wall above the table isn't big enough for all of them. If he stacks them on his desk, the window won't open. And the top of the wardrobe is already occupied by his empty suitcase. It looks like he'll have to sort through them and put the ones he needs first on the shelf so they're ready at hand, while the rest can stay in their boxes. He decides to postpone the task until tomorrow, however, because the ceiling light is too dim. He puts the boxes of books on the bed for now to make room and begins pacing back and forth in order to outline the planning calendar in his mind. It seems unfair to calculate only the number of pages written. Days when he reads a lot but doesn't write anything will look like they were idly spent.

Hence, two columns are not enough, he'll have to create a third for the number of hours worked. Calculating and recording this number in the evening will boost his morale in the daytime.

He lays out paper, pen, and ruler for drawing up the calendar. But first he needs to go to the bathroom. This is located next to Frau Erika's room. It even has a bathtub. He checks the water temperature and decides to take a bath. Songs from *The Cousin from Nowhere* provide him with entertainment while he washes. Frau Erika occasionally sings along. He later hears her leave her room and walk downstairs. His curiosity is piqued by voices and noises when he gets out of the bath. There's no window in the hallway, so he has to walk down half a flight of stairs. The farmyard outside is illuminated. Max and Gabi are busy in front of the cowsheds with milk cans, pails, and rags. Frau Erika, in fur coat and hat, has two milk jugs filled, pays, lets out a shrill "Here Kitty, Kitty!" then walks over to the garage, where her "sweet little bunnies"—the cats—are waiting for her. From the cowshed come the sounds of clanging chains and contented lowing. The wind drives scattered snowflakes through the light of the lamps. Thilde is nowhere in sight.

Viktor's room seems even colder to him now after taking a warm bath. He slips on two sweaters, one on top of the other. By the time he decides to give his calendar the heading "Performance Check" his knees are cold. He takes the boxes of books off the bed, slides them underneath it, wraps the blanket around his legs, and hops back to his desk. Placing the ruler on the page, he draws the first horizontal line. Then he pauses and listens; rapid footsteps mount the stairs and hurry to the garret where the gardener lives. Voices can be heard but are unintelligible. The footsteps come back downstairs and halt in front of Frau Erika's door.

"Is Tita with you?"

Viktor hears the lisping *s* and rises to his feet. He forgets, however, that his legs are bound, and falls over—luckily onto the bed.

"Herr Kösling," the voice calls out from the stairs, "is my grandmother with you?"

"No!" he cries out, flinging off the blanket and rushing to the door. But the hallway is empty by the time he gets there. From the stairwell window he sees Thilde scurry across the yard, first to the cowshed, then to the kitchen. When he leaves his room a second time, Sebastian is coming down. The stairs quake beneath his step. Viktor seems to shrink before him—a feeling he knows from encounters with his father. The gardener would prefer to walk past with a simple greeting, but Viktor holds out his hand and offers his name. In a voice that's surprisingly squeaky coming from a mass of facial hair, Viktor is asked if he really is, as rumor would have it, the son of Kösling the Great.

Viktor has plenty of experience with people who ask questions like that. He can usually tell by their facial expression or their tone of voice what a positive response will elicit: admiration or cool reserve. The admirers normally receive a modest "Yes," the reserved he answers with "I am but never mind." But when someone asks and their face betrays nothing (because it's buried behind a beard, for instance), their voice sounds neutral, or when their choice of words might be construed as ironic, such a person gets a "Like it or loathe it, there's nothing I can do about it."

This answer pleases Sebastian, who laughs and promptly proceeds on his way. Viktor, who has a yearning for conversation, is once again left standing alone on the drafty stairs in front of the window, outside of which things are livening up. The gardener has barely made it to the yard when Gabi and Thomas show up. The twins disappear from Viktor's field of view as soon as Max opens the garage door. Then Thilde steps into the circle of light and Viktor goes to fetch his coat from his room. By the time he arrives in the yard, Thilde has left it again already. Max asks Viktor to get in the car, which is soon traversing Dead Man's Road, lurching and lunging its way forward. After a slew of curses that are new to Viktor, Max explains to his passenger that he has no intention of carrying on this nonsense much longer: he's the head administrator here and doesn't work at a loony bin.

TITA'S TRIP

That Tita was born at New Glory and not in Klein-Kietz has to do with the import duties on wool. When they were repealed at the end of the last century and the market was flooded with cheap (duty-free) Australian wool, the lord of the manor in Görtz, who had hitherto made the bulk of his livelihood breeding sheep, went bankrupt and had to sell off land. Tita's father, the youngest son of an innkeeper from Klein-Kietz in the Neumark (now part of Poland), jumped at the opportunity. He bought up two hundred acres for a song and built his farmstead with its extravagant name smack in the middle of it. The photograph of him hanging up in Tita's room shows a man looking exactly the way you would imagine a parvenu from back then, or nowadays for that matter. The family grave he had built in Prötz cemetery towers over the rest. Tita keeps it looking immaculate. There's room enough for her, then it'll be full.

Tita's brothers were killed in the first war, her sons in the second, and Lüderitz, her ever ailing husband, only outlived the shock of reorganization of the countryside by a matter of weeks. The buildings were rented out to the Ministry, and Tita, no longer young but hale and hearty, ran the home for a dozen years.

Apart from being hard of hearing, she's still in good shape physically; it's only her mental faculties that are starting to fail her now and then. She mixes up time—the time of day and of her life in general—and takes Sebastian, for example, to be her servant, giving him orders to get to work threshing. Or she'll wander through the house in the middle of the night beating her cane on the doors and calling everyone lazy bums for sleeping through the morning hours. Once she even let Max's cows out and drove them to a spot that used to be pasture. Other times she'll become alarmed that the house isn't blacked out and will start hanging blankets in the windows. Then, moments later, she'll be back to normal and will laugh in embarrassment if you tell her what she's been up to.

Her vagaries are often the topic of kitchen conversation. Olga is worried about the bottles of propane gas in the kitchen. If, in a moment of derangement, Tita would decide to go after one of those, she says, they'd all be blown to smithereens. Yet she vigorously protests when Max suggests (gingerly, so as not to upset Thilde) taking Tita and, as he puts it, carting her off to an asylum. "Pay attention," Olga says to Püppi, "to what your papa is saying. When you're all grown up someday and he's grown old, you'll know how to get rid of him."

They naturally lower their voices when talking about Tita in her presence, and avoid looking her way. Yet it sometimes happens that Tita will suddenly jump to her feet and say, "I'd best be going now, so you can bad-mouth me without my bothering you." Olga will then shout in her ear, "That's not true, Tita, no one's putting you down," to which Thilde adds, "Aw, c'mon, sit down and eat, it's no fun without you." Tita will then sit back down and tell amusing tales from the days of her youth, so that everyone laughs and no one can imagine that in a few days or weeks she'll have another spell.

You can tell that one is coming by her nervousness. She walks to and fro, rubs her hands, and has a restless look in her eyes. If you talk to her, she'll answer as if you were a stranger. In moments like these it's possible that she'll bolt and never come back. If you hold her back, she'll acquiesce, but will just be waiting for an unguarded moment.

Viktor learns in the car that today is just such a day. "She's on one of her trips again," Max comments, grumbling first about Thilde, who won't admit that Tita's condition can only worsen, then about the snow, which is now falling heavily from an inky sky.

They cover the villages of Görtz, Prötz, and Arndtsdorf, slowly due to the icy roads. There's no one on the streets as far as the eye can see. Viktor soon regrets having offered to help. His presence is superfluous, his only task being to listen to Max. And everything that Max says is larded with obscenities. At first Viktor marvels at Max's inventiveness in this regard, but after a while the repetitions start to wear on him. His own attempt to add something folksy and vulgar about the weather doesn't go down so well. His efforts to divert the conversation from Tita to Thilde likewise fall flat. Max is too busy articulating his anger, which, coming from him, sounds like this: "Boy, does that make my blood boil!" He says this several times. Viktor, recalling Max's humble civility when he arrived, feels uneasy next to a driver who can't control his emotions.

Three times in each village (nine times in all), Max gets out to ask Tita's acquaintances if they've seen her anywhere. He leaves Viktor behind in the freezing car, alone with his thoughts, which are not about the snow, the raging storm, or his dissertation but about himself.

Particularly when he's tired (and this he is, increasingly so, despite the cold), he sometimes manages to come up with figures of thought that he likes to call autologies, a term he coined himself. These have nothing to do with the automobile he's sitting in, but with the foreign root word for "self," which has a double meaning for him: autologies are thoughts that he alone thinks (that no one has thought before him or for him) as well as thoughts about himself. His efforts to this end—performed in a state of semidreaming but nonetheless yielding precise results—are called autologizing. It often keeps him in bed in the morning and can shorten the monotony of driving on the autobahn at night. The essence of autologies is that their fruits cannot be shared with others; they only exist for him. Although they're neither language, image, nor sound, he can hear them and see them. For as long as they last they are independent entities, so to speak—objects of thought, distinct, vivid, logical, and clearly delineated, *Gesamtkunstwerke* providing new variations on a single, inexhaustible theme: himself, from varied perspectives.

The autology being perfected in the cooling car—while Max is calling at the inn (with the misleading name of Lakeview) in Arndtsdorf, where he lingers longer than usual—could be given the title "Viktor and Women." It was triggered by self-pity. Viktor, who in effect can't afford to spare a single hour of his precious writing time, sits by idly, fatigued and freezing, with nothing but a thin sheet of metal protecting him from the elements, and this not because he's eager to lend a helping hand but because his curiosity compelled him to try to get a glimpse of the face of a certain Thilde, who until now has been distinguished only by her lisping sibilants, her young age, and her gender. From her it's only a short jaunt down the path of contemplation to other female figures. If he were to paint a picture in his mind, it would depict a number of girls and women (to be more precise: eight) arranged in such a manner that Viktor's portrait, looming large behind them, would only shine through in places; indeed, it would appear as though Viktor consisted of nothing but Inges, Elkes, and Ritas. The male theme, if the autology were to be heard as music, would be lost among the many female melodies, eventually disappearing entirely, dissolving into them—which, if all of this were written out, would go something like this: having long since gotten used to others making decisions for him, he's the opposite of a seducer: that is to say, the ever seducible. His feelings for women are like a reflector, sending off only as much warmth and light as he himself receives. He could never be unfaithful; he could only be *made* unfaithful. He's the ideal lover, always conforming to the image of him his respective partner has created.

His inner self-portrait (along with the growing suspicion that active curiosity doesn't suit him) fades once Max returns. Viktor warms up again, from outside and within, when Max starts the engine and pulls a bottle of corn schnapps out of his pocket. He opens it, puts it to his lips, then hands it to Viktor, who can barely resist the temptation to wipe it clean with his hankie. The liquor's unpleasant burn doesn't prevent him from letting out an appreciative "Ahhh!" when removing the bottle from his lips. Max, too, finds that the booze is just what he needs, takes another slug, and only then announces that his change in spirits is not only due to the alcohol: he found out where Tita is by phoning from the restaurant. In the blink of an eye (and at an alarming speed, it seems to Viktor) they're on their way there, through virgin snow-white fields, then through woods, where branches bend under the burden of snow.

Potholes, which can't be seen in the darkness and snow but certainly can be felt, are no reason for Max to slow down. His destination is Schwedenow, a village in the woods, of which Viktor only gets a glimpse since Tita is in the very first house. Having asked for directions like an out-of-towner, she's sitting now in a toasty kitchen, waiting for the mail van to Klein-Kietz.

"It's about time you came!" she snaps at Max, "they're waiting in Kietz." She hasn't taken off her coat or scarf and didn't drink the tea she was offered. She remains silent in the car, doesn't even answer when Viktor asks her a question, and complains only about the darkness. She becomes restless whenever the tempo slackens. When Max stops the car and gets out to check the depth of the snow, she shouts after him, "Get a move on, it's high time!"

Along the way, Viktor pictures himself leading the fugitive grandmother to a grateful Thilde. No sooner has the vehicle pulled up to the garage than Viktor is outside opening the door for Tita. But the latter insists they're not there yet and remains seated. He doesn't have long to reason with her, because Max needs his help: snowdrifts are blocking the garage door. Thilde comes and whisks Tita away into the house while the two men are busy shoveling. All that Viktor sees is Thilde's slender silhouette against the lamplight. The bottle Max once again hands him repulses him this time. Twice he declines, then finishes off the appreciable rest of it after all—because Max so wills it.

The effects are felt as he reaches his room. Always one for orderliness, even with a clouded consciousness, he puts paper, pen, and ruler into the desk drawer. In bed he tries to contemplate the outline of his dissertation but doesn't make it beyond the idea of marking the introduction with a capital *A*. His zeal for work is hindered by sleep.

Snow and Grog

"You would have made a good philosopher," Viktor says the following evening to Sebastian, the gardener, in his garret, which is small and extremely warm. He says this with a heavy tongue and lips that are just about numb after a few too many glasses of grog. They've reached the end of a long discussion about order, which has become the topic of conversation by virtue of its being disturbed. Prussia, which should be uppermost in Viktor's mind, is mentioned only in passing (as a "power of order"). The discussion is about order per se: the order one loves, the order one keeps, the order people are accustomed to, the order of everyday life, of society, and of nature.

This last, the order of nature, has become the center of attention thanks to the cold and snow. What the newspapers (undelivered for three days) call inclement weather sets in at night. Viktor speaks of catastrophe in his conversations with others, while deep down inside him a mounting sense of cheerfulness takes hold, which he does his best to hide—even from himself. With the love of order drilled into him so well, he can't admit the freedom he feels when this order suddenly begins to waver. Thus, the joy that stirs him he interprets as courage in the face of calamity, as a chance to prove his mettle.

His first reaction upon waking, of course, is to be appalled by the cold. His hand gets a taste of it, reaching for the wristwatch on the nightstand. Since the lower part of the window is snowed in and the upper part is covered with hoarfrost, the room (at nine o'clock) is still half dark. He turns on the radio and hears reports about chaos on the roads, trains unable to run, villages cut off by snow, coal shortages and power outages. New Glory still has electricity—luckily, he says, disappointed. Before heading to the bathroom, he makes a peephole in the frost with his breath. The landscape he sees is a hazy blur, the snow still falling heavily. He hears sounds from the yard (metal scraping on concrete) and voices (Thilde's among them). He's eager to join the others in their snow removal efforts. Olga provides him with breakfast and rustic attire.

Everyone is sporting a peculiar costume to protect themselves from the easterly wind and subzero temperatures. Yet the only outfit that causes hilarity is Viktor's. When Thilde hides her face behind a scarf so that only her eyes (brown with a touch of yellow, Viktor is quick to discern) can be seen beneath her hat, it is no more than an understandable desire to keep warm. But when the son of Kösling pulls a pom-pom hat (Manuela's) over his ears and puts on a padded coat and felt boots, the result is both comical and moving at once.

"People," says Sebastian later, not counting himself among them, because he's the kind of person who can observe, explain, and look through them—"people don't really like it when someone who belongs somewhere else pretends to be like them. They sense the arrogance behind it. Because, if you think about it, 'I'm just like you' basically means 'In addition to what *I* am, I'm also what *you* are on top of it, in other words, *more* than you.' Experience has taught them to be suspicious of that kind of thing. Order requires segregation, and someone who pretends to ignore it has ulterior motives. But when a lummox like you comes along," Sebastian continues, the "you" meaning Viktor, his conversation partner, "they're able to smile and chuckle, because the farce they're witnessing only goes to show them that you can't just become like them when you want to—which obviously flatters them."

The clever gardener is right. But he's wrong about Viktor. Viktor is no lummox, he's just playing the part out of fear of not living up to demands. He acts like a bozo to avoid the threat of being despised as a failure. He gains the sympathy of others by admiring them. By voluntarily placing himself on the lowest rungs, his slightest improvement is honored with praise. While it's true that Max, Olga, Tita, and Thilde may laugh at him, they're grateful to him for the chance to lecture him and for the feeling of self-respect this gives them.

"Not like that, like this," says Thilde, showing him how to hold the shovel in order to get more out of less effort. She does so with a lisp so lovely that Viktor can only pine for more. But nothing comes of it. Tita (her mental faculties again intact) has used the emergency to tighten the reins and regain authority. She orders Viktor to the gate. His chore, together with Sebastian, is to clear away a man-high snowdrift. All they're doing for now is clearing a path into an impassable snowy waste, but at some point the snowplow from Görtz will come, restoring access to the main road. Sebastian and Viktor have a good day's work cut out for them. Although often taking breaks from shoveling, their conversation seldom flags.

From the topic of snow, which hasn't let up yet, they promptly move on to Tita, a mystery to Viktor, though one that Sebastian thinks he can solve. Tita, he says, is a victim of order, and order, if not his greatest foe, is something Sebastian despises, as Viktor soon learns. If order is a necessity, as Kösling's son throws in, that's still no reason to worship it. The call of nature is also inevitable without becoming sacred; how could it, when even the dullest mind can see through the mechanisms behind it. Systems of order of whatever kind, on the other hand, are obscured behind a smoke screen of incense, allowing you to worship but not analyze them. Analysis is tantamount to blasphemy, since every order has its gods, its one God, or its higher system of laws to which it acts as representative. Anyone who wants to be more than just a cog in the machinery of order, however, and who wants to have a mind of his own will try to lift his head above the clouds of incense.

Sebastian's shovel is idle when he says this, his arm propped on top of it. He's standing upright, his shaggy head towering well above Viktor's, neatly supporting his vivid metaphor. Viktor is doubly impressed: by Sebastian, who can talk so well, and by Viktor, who moves him to do so. Once again, his ability to inspire the trust of others has stood the test. Sympathy can be won by displaying an interest, which is easy enough because he does have an interest—less for what he calls philosophical matters, more for the personal issues the philosophical ones boil down to. If the conversation has gone from snow to Tita to order, he ponders, they'll eventually wind up discussing Thilde, as long as he doesn't distract him. He therefore takes care not to disrupt the gardener's meandering thoughts but goes with the flow, bobbing his head.

Long is the route his thoughts traverse. They even delve into word origins, insinuating that these sometimes give rise to what the words signify. The Latin *ordinare*, for instance, Sebastian cites by way of example (and at this point Viktor and every reader will ask themselves how a gardener living in the remote corner of a village in the Mark Brandenburg knows a thing like that; this will be revealed later on by the gardener himself, who is in the process of doing so now, albeit indirectly, by talking about the order in which Viktor and the reader are accustomed to thinking)—the Latin *ordinare*, from which the semantically related German words are derived, means "to put into rows," and that, says Sebastian, is what order is all about: putting people and things into first, second, and third rows, lining them up and assigning them ranks. There's no need to remind yourself of the order of merit you're awarded for loyalty in serving the public order, and of the fraternal order that unites the chosen custodians of law and order at the top. There's no need when the order—the command—is in your ear. The essence of order is compulsion. Compulsion creates and maintains it.

Sebastian's hair, which no scissors come near and which takes the place of a hat, waves in the wind when he solemnly proclaims that compulsion, by nature, is an abomination to man. Man's will is not to be a number in the third row or an accountant; all he wants is to be himself. To make him compatible with order, then, he has to be domesticated. This is accomplished by bending his will, preferably to such an extent that he produces the compulsion on his own through what is commonly called a sense of duty and ambition.

Viktor, who whether working or resting always positions himself with a view to the yard and its snow-sweeping women, briefly loses track of them when he hears the word *ambition*. Ambition, he confesses to Sebastian, is something he's had problems with ever since his childhood. Apparently he wasn't properly domesticated. He always considered it a flaw. If it's true, though, what Sebastian says, it seems there's no reason for him to be ashamed of it.

Although not exactly expecting praise, Viktor at least expected Sebastian to take an interest in his inner life. But Viktor is disappointed. Instead of commenting on his confession, Sebastian merely resumes his lecture, touching now on historical matters, which Viktor doesn't follow, being more interested in the yard. Working has warmed up Thilde. She stands next to Olga, chatting while removing the scarf from her face. Alas, she turns her back to Viktor, but she's bound to turn around at some point, which is exactly what he's waiting for. He regards her hair in the meantime, visible under the fur hat she's wearing. A red ribbon holds it together at the nape of her neck.

The lecture has since gone from general to specific. Sebastian now gets down to examples, to personal matters, to Tita, and to the lecturer himself, Sebastian Eymann, with a *y*, who experienced home-grown compulsion the hard way. An emotionally healthy child, he wanted at first to be Robinson Crusoe, then an explorer, and later a forester—that is, until the domestication process took effect and he strived instead of living. The goal was good grades. From best of the class he went on to become a top scholar and elite soldier. By the time he was thirty, he was head of his department, in charge of foreign trade in plastics and elastics, obedient, agile, and principled, industrious and restless, fenced in mentally, impoverished emotionally: solid second row with first-row prospects. Horrifying! Sebastian grimaces with disgust, shoveling more vigorously in an effort to slough it off. It causes him to lose his breath but he keeps on talking all the same. He coins phrases like "diligence syndrome" and "impotency with district heating" to describe his former state; he comes up with metaphors involving parrots and ashes, galley boats and mental garbage. Yet when and where and how the great turning point in his life occurred, this he leaves unsaid. In any event, it happened—accompanied by the realization that order these days is so construed that if you care about your own well-being, rather than climb you'd do better to drop, preferably into the fourth row, which is to say: drop out.

Things have been good since Sebastian came to this realization and began to act upon it. He's been here a year already, officially as a gardener, in reality as a manual laborer, a man-of-all-work, sometimes loafing, sometimes toiling, independent, contemplative, free of cares. Here at New Glory he's regained a sense of what he is and what he's capable of. Today, for example: the wind, the snow, the cold, the clean air, the work before you both meaningful and tangible, your own body which you can feel again, the sleep in the evening that's sure to come! Sebastian is not afraid to call it happiness. If this is not happiness, what is?

Or the Back Bush! He sticks his shovel into the wall of snow they've piled up already and trudges outside the gate. Viktor is obliged to follow, as much as it pains him on account of the view. They walk along the front of the house toward Prötz, the wind at their backs, snow up to their knees, not far, just to the corner of the wall. There's not much to see: a strip of snow-covered field no wider than New Glory and slightly sloping, bordered on the right by Dead Man's Road, behind it, hardly visible, trees, above them dusky clouds. That's the Back Bush, formerly Lüderitz farmland, uneconomical (too small) for today's heavy machinery, long abandoned as wasteland, overgrown along the roadside with a prickly wilderness of plum trees that spreads from year to year. Tita's father planted the plum trees along Dead Man's Road. Their gloomy ruins now rise from the snow. Their roots, however, are indestructible. You have to dig them up, otherwise they just keep sprouting back up again. The scrubby trees aren't exactly pretty, what with the damage caused by wild animals. Even less pretty, though, is the garbage strewn in the field, covered now by snow. Screened from view by the wall and the windowless barn, the occasional passerby on his way to the nearby dump is tempted to unload his cart before reaching his destination. Tita becomes infuriated when she finds new piles of broken glass or ash. Whenever people from Görtz drive past the house with a load of trash, she runs outside and stands guard. Only when the vehicle has disappeared behind the cemetery trees does she go back in.

In the springtime, says Sebastian, he'll be turning this eyesore into a park of his own design, the trees and bushes have already been ordered, the Ministry gets to foot the bill. Viktor learns about the project's various stages: hauling away the garbage, rooting out the scrub, plowing up the ground, marking out and leveling the paths, planting the trees. In his mind, they grow like lightning, says Sebastian. Lying in his attic room in the evening, he can already see creepers climbing up the old wall, flowering bushes, benches, Dead Man's Road as a shady avenue. There's no work that compares to making plans of your own, and that's exactly what everyone's being denied these days. "Now do you get what I'm saying?"

The question is so sudden that Viktor can't think of anything to say but "Of course." Yes, he understands this big man well. His enthusiasm is one he can share. He's especially impressed by the expression "free of cares." He has already lived nearly half his life and not once, as far as he can remember, has he ever used it. What a paltry existence he's led up till now: dependent, far from nature, full of cares. With contempt he thinks of the books awaiting him in his room. What's a doctorate compared to a shady avenue you've planted all on your own? Nothing! How sad the stuffy air of a study compared with the wind driving snow into their eyes on the brief walk back! A breath of freedom, thinks Viktor, but doesn't say so because he'd have to interrupt Sebastian, who's moved on to the mystery of Tita and, with that, is back to the theme of order—order and the toll it takes.

The images change this time. Domestication becomes veneer; Klein-Kietz, where Tita was allowed to be a child, is called paradise, and he no longer talks about first, second, and third rows but about inside and outside, meaning squeezed into the mold of order or outside of it entirely.

The storyteller's knowledge is astonishing. Life at New Glory circa 1895 is as familiar to him as if he had lived it. He knows about the initial difficulties back when Tita's father was *Bauherr und Bauer,* builder and farmer in one, knows what happened to the first rye harvest in the still barnless farmyard, and how they lived before the house went up. Viktor isn't sure where Sebastian learned the specifics and doesn't ask him either, because that would sound like he doubted its truthfulness. He says only, "Aha!" "So that's what it was like!" and "Interesting!" while waiting for the granddaughter.

But grandmother is still a child for the time being, one of four, already a half orphan at the age of two. Her mother died soon after the new farm on Dead Man's Road was completed. Her father had no acquaintances in the area and a second wife was hard to come by. The older sons were able to help out on the farm a little and stayed at New Glory. Tita was sent back to the Neumark, to Klein-Kietz, where her grandmother raised her at the Good Friend Inn—devoid of any discipline, totally free and unburdened, because her grandmother had withdrawn into her retirement quarters, no longer had any obligations on the farm or in the guesthouse, and saved Tita from having any either. The two of them lived, as it were, beyond the reach of order, "on the outside" as Sebastian calls it, in the tone of voice others might use for Freedom, Work, or God.

How hard it was to take this child of nature and belatedly coat her with a uniform veneer once her grandmother passed away, this he makes clear in a detailed fashion. At Gabi's age, twelve years old, Tita was sent back to the paternal prison. Five years later she made her final attempt to flee, then it was over and she suppressed her yearning for the paradise of Klein-Kietz. The veneer was glued in place, and she no longer noticed that her soul was suffocating underneath it. Her brothers never came back from the war, Tita got married, had children, and held the reins for a lifetime, first on the farm, then at the home, until the memory of her true existence was lost, intruding in her dreams at most. But now the self-constraint hammered into her has lost its meaning, and she's slowly starting to come around. "You people," says Sebastian, setting down his shovel and giving Viktor a nasty look, "you people all talk about degeneration. I'd say the veneer is cracking, and the individual underneath is finally reemerging."

Viktor decides to hold his tongue. He puts on a pensive face but adds a nod just in case to keep the giant in check. This final remark was uncalled-for. Degeneration may have crossed his mind, but all he ever mentioned was the mystery of Tita. This has now been solved by Sebastian—how fascinating!—but Viktor has been waiting to hear about someone else.

"Hilde, or what's-her-name, is her granddaughter?" he asks, but all he receives in reply is "Uh-huh."

He has long since abandoned his observation point at the gate. The object he longs to see is no longer in his field of view. The women, except for Tita, have all gone into the house. Only Max is left sweeping, and this with half his strength, since he's using one of his arms to warm Püppi, who's had enough of the snow for now. Viktor, too, is dissatisfied. His arms are stiff, his back hurts, his hands and feet are freezing. He leaves the rest of the work to Sebastian. In the lee of the house, he watches and listens. The gardener is back to talking about trees, the ones that will shade the road someday. Some that he mentions Viktor has never even heard of before. A certain variety is out of the question because of the barren soil, another is too wind-sensitive; this kind doesn't grow fast enough for Sebastian, that kind is impossible to get.

Viktor remembers the warm tiled stove. One shouldn't get carried away, he thinks, trying to lend a hand. Having made up his mind to go inside, Tita suddenly appears at the gate. For the first time she takes notice of Herr Kösling, welcomes him as a guest, thanks him for his help. At times she can be rather ceremonial. Frau Erika follows close behind, full of praise for Kösling's son. Olga calls them in to lunch. The dining-room table is set for him alone. Köpke is roaming the woods. Frau Erika sits down at the table with Viktor, spoons up bits of cottage cheese, and talks about the plight of birds. She needs a feeder for her windowsill. Viktor, who knows hammers and saws only from hearsay, promises to build her one. Gabi, Manuela, and Thomas get home late from school. An argument ensues about the height of the snowdrifts they had to wade through. The streets are still passable, so they pin their hopes on tomorrow. If the weather report is right, there won't be any school buses running.

Viktor scarfs down his meal and steals into his room. The stove has been stoked, his bed is made. He sits at his desk for a couple of minutes, then his eyes begin to droop. Without undressing, he crawls into bed and sleeps until suppertime. Sebastian invites him to stop by in the evening. They sit in his room under the roof for hours, guzzling grog, hot, strong, and sweet, next to the stove. Not wanting to ask about the granddaughter directly, Viktor asks about Tita's daughter. He doesn't learn much. She was never a good mother to Thilde and has limited her duties to sending packages. The other questions Sebastian dodges. And soon his questions cease altogether; Viktor is now too far gone to come up with harmless ones. He hears himself laughing, without being in a laughing mood. Sebastian's speeches are mere noises to him, like the blustering winds that sweep the ridge of the roof. He repeatedly resolves, then and there, to rise up out of his chair, but only does so at Sebastian's behest.

The stairs from the garret are steep and narrow, dimly illuminated by the hall light from the first floor. Viktor descends them like a toddler, careful to place both feet on each step. He manages fine until about the middle, at which point he senses that his legs will no longer obey him. It's no use clutching the railing either, his limbs do what they want with him. They want rest, hence Viktor sits. His head is leaning on something wooden, an edge pressing painfully into his forehead. His eyes shut on their own. A singular effort is required to open them.

He's unaware, later on, how long he needed to open them. He can't recall the reason either (probably a noise). The little work his brain is capable of is just enough to hold in place what crosses his field of vision. First the socks, gray and coarsely woven, then eight to ten inches of bare leg above them, which vanishes under cloth. Viktor's head is leaning against the railing posts and he has to raise it a little bit before recognizing that the cloth (red-and-black-striped) is a bathrobe. A hand carrying slippers enters his field of view. A sound ensues that's too quiet to be called a scream—it's a scream that dies before it's really there, a stillborn one, so to speak. It doesn't cross the person's lips (which Viktor glimpses only moments later), it remains an inner scream, barely audible. The eyes betray what triggered it (fear), the same eyes Viktor encountered this morning. He doesn't get to study them though. For no sooner has he lifted his head enough to where he can make out a hairline than already he sees the hair from behind—dark, no longer tied back but undone. The apparition escapes his view as swiftly and soundlessly as it came.

Viktor can distinctly remember the face's details the next morning (he's up early after sleeping poorly), but he still can't piece them together into a coherent picture. The mouth, preserved in his memory as particularly full of expression, is much too big in relation to the eyes, the forehead is missing entirely, and the brown skin, tautly stretched over bone—this you'd expect to find in India, certainly not at New Glory.

The Omnipotence of Desire

Never and nowhere are Viktor's thoughts as clear and ordered as they are in the morning in bed. The blanket is a breeding ground for thoughts. If he lies under it long enough, his brooding produces the finest decisions. Three of them are reached on his second morning of working vacation. The first concerns his body, the second his work, the third his communication with others. The decisions are precipitated by his poor state of body and mind. Besides a headache from the grog, he's plagued by pains in his back and limbs from all the unaccustomed shoveling. Added to this is the pall cast over his spirits by the pressure to perform, which can't be battled without some kind of inner reinforcement. This, however, has to come from others. He therefore resolves, first of all, to not touch another snow shovel, weather notwithstanding, but second, only his typewriter, and third, to focus on a soul that will warm and invigorate his own. He has one in mind.

Viktor has no experience in snaring souls, plenty though in being ensnared. And from this he derives the method he'll use—not by, say, swapping the usual starting positions, but by creating the proper setup. He'll hunt his prey by posing as the hunted, transforming his prey into the hunter. This means knowing how to qualify as a catch. He'll need to engage in targeted communication, in all directions. His first attempt at communication, with Sebastian, was seemingly fruitless, but on closer inspection wasn't at all. Because information is sometimes supplied by dint of its being denied.

The fact that the gardener probably already possesses the object of Viktor's desire doesn't discourage him. Rather, it spurs him on. What worries him is the skin he glimpsed. It's no coincidence it reminded him of India, a place he's never been. His only experience with an Indian woman was in a hotel and ended rather awkwardly for him. Having misunderstood the feelings she expressed in English, he volunteered a service that hadn't been requested of him. Ever since then, brown skin has been to him a symbol of unattainability and foreignness.

Luckily, the swarthy girl at New Glory speaks German, albeit with a speech impediment. "Not like that, like this!" she lisped to him the previous morning, then cried out voicelessly on account of him at night. He's lodged himself in her mind, then; now he'll have to concentrate on making his presence felt. Without letting on to his intent to conquer, which could conceivably scare her off, he somehow has to express his interest in her. Because lavishing your attentions on a woman invariably means one thing: directing her attention toward you.

The weather facilitates his resolutions. Although cold and windy, it's finally stopped snowing, yesterday evening, in fact. The new snow is easy to sweep from the paths. Sebastian is already working on it as Viktor makes for the dining room. Thus, he can easily honor his resolution not to take up a shovel again.

The opportunity to communicate presents itself at breakfast. Viktor's place at the table in the empty dining room is laid with cup, plate, butter, and jam, but he has to make a trip to the kitchen to get his coffee and eggs. He finds Olga there alone. She's sitting at the main table, smoking and peeling potatoes, a glass of liquid, clear as water, next to her. Viktor's coffee and eggs are ready. Not only does Olga serve him, she entertains him as well. He eats and drinks, occasionally tossing in a question; she talks and smokes, both profusely. Although she hides her alcohol consumption, she's proud of being a smoker. Whether walking, standing, or sitting, Viktor is told, she's always puffing away—forty to sixty a day, the first and last in bed. It starts, she says, obeying her compulsion to repeat herself, before she even gets up and doesn't let up until the evening, right before she dozes off. Two to three packs are her workday ration, less on Sunday because of her nap. She holds up her nicotine-stained fingers like trophies while baring her teeth, which she refers to as "smoked."

Viktor can smell the schnapps on her breath and feels embarrassed. Not wanting to let on, he saves himself with a compliment. He praises her hands, which hardly surprises her, she acknowledges earnestly. Indeed, Herr Kösling is right: she has every reason to show them, there's no need to hide them, you can tell they've seen better days. The sigh that fills the ensuing pause is rightly construed by her listener as the prelude to her life story. He lends his ear in the hope that by inserting encouraging questions he'll hear a shorter one afterward, one that interests him more—a short story rather than a novel.

That's exactly how Olga refers to her life: a novel. Someone with a nimble pen, she says, need only write it down; he'd have it made, because sad stories sell best. He'd just have to know how to tell it properly (thinks Viktor). The way Olga relates it you can barely sort through the jumble of names and facts. Her references to time are wholly obscure. Instead of supplying a date or a person's age, it's "after Mama died," "before my second marriage," or "back then in court." The phases of her life have men's names, and when she talks about playing piano, she always means the prime of her youth. By what he can gather from the welter of information, all the men she's ever loved have been devils, dragging her from one misfortune to the next until she finally landed at the bottom, with archdemon Max, who not only runs a black-market car business and beats his children but has other women on the side, one in Trebatsch and two in Buckow. "But his days are numbered," she concludes. "It's over with him. His time is up."

Olga looks like her mission in life is to embody Sebastian's theory of self-compulsion. She sits in her chair, stiff und unmoving, and barely parts her narrow lips when speaking. Even when she threatens "that scoundrel" or says "I went and reported him!" her voice remains unchanged. Viktor is feeling inwardly cramped by the time that Olga leaves. Just listening to her has made him rigid. Frau Erika will loosen him up!

She gently opens the door to her room as Viktor comes up the stairs. Peering left and right down the hall, she seizes Viktor by the hand and pulls him into her chamber. She calls him "my prince" and, clasping his other hand, stands face-to-face with him, as though they were about to begin a round dance. She's beaming. "The two of us," she stage-whispers in an artifically high-pitched, almost singsong voice, "the two of us, the prince and his fairy godmother, have a common secret! One that we have to keep. Shall we?"

Frau Erika has done herself up for Viktor. She's wearing a high-necked dirndl dress with a little white apron over it. The ribbon festooning her freshly curled hair is blue-and-red-checked, just like the dress. She's applied her makeup quite skillfully; the only thing old about her is her eyes and the little bit of neck not covered by her silk scarf. It's not hard for Viktor to smile back at her radiantly and (since no spectators are present) to play along with her little theater. "Indeed, sweet fairy," he answers, singing it like she did, "let us make a vow together"—then, well aware of the comic effect, immediately adds in a normal tone that first she has to let him in on the secret.

Frau Erika laughs out loud, lets go of his hands, and plops into a chair. Viktor pulls up another one and takes a seat across from her. She offers him coffee, scoots the crystal candy dish in his direction, then gets up and turns on the fireplace. She puts on a record and, swaying in time to "White Horse Inn" with a mischievous look in her eyes, says only "Gypsy girl."

Viktor knows right away who and what she's referring to but doesn't know how to react. He plays the innocent in order to gain time, puts on a brooding face, shrugs his shoulders, and says, "Beg your pardon?" Frau Erika explains. She and Helgalein (who comes every Sunday to supply her with good-quality coffee) have a special name for everyone at the home. Max, because of his sky-blue eyes, they call Hans Albers after the famous actor, Olga is Smoked Eel, Sebastian is the Elephant Baby, and Tita (at this point Erika raises her fist to her chin and indicates a long, pointy one) King Thrushbeard. "Now do you understand?"

"Of course!" Viktor shouts, enamored by the sisters' sense of humor. He makes a how-could-I-be-such-a-dimwit gesture, smacking his forehead repeatedly with the palm of his hand (and really coming out of his shell in the process). "Now I know who you mean. Hilde, or what's-her-name, the granddaughter."

Viktor finally learns that her real name is Klothilde and that the old-fashioned name—straight from the prop room, so to say—is thanks to her grandmother. Frau Erika asked Thilde's mother about it, who once in a blue moon makes the trip over for one of her obligatory visits. She was only seventeen when the baby came, unwanted, and was happy that Tita took it off her hands and assumed the role of provider—providing the shameful name as well, a name which is neither pretty nor appropriate for that matter. Nobody knows where Klothilde got her Gypsy-like appearance. There was none of it in the Lüderitz family. The father, they say, weighed two hundred pounds, a baker blond and pale. He was already a grandfather four times over when he violated his shopgirl in the heat of his bakery. The exertion was too much for him, Frau Erika presumes. He was dead by the time the swarthy child was born.

Even when she's sitting, Frau Erika is in motion. If she happens to mention long black hair, her hand shows how it drapes the shoulders. Both arms are needed to encircle the two-hundred-pounder's waist. And when it's the seventeen-year-old mother's turn, lean Frau Erika is the picture of a pregnant woman. Her face is aimed at the ceiling when thinking, she turns her head to the side when listening, and her hands are always involved when she laughs. She turns the music up or down, trills along to a song or two, and occasionally recites a line: "Happiness is close at hand!" She pours him coffee and offers cookies, the crystal dish in outstretched arms, entreating him with earnest tenderness: "You must eat, my prince!" She's brisk and cheerful, silly and thoughtful. She's playing the little girl, and Viktor is playing right along. He doesn't dodge her stare; when she bends forward, he leans in. With a twitch of his nostrils he indicates that her perfume is pleasing and doesn't so much as flinch when her hands touch his knee. Her mouth is close to his when, again in a singing tone, she says, "I've long known what you found out last night."

She leans back in her chair again. Now he, too, can sit back and relax. She talks—hands on the nape of her neck, gazing at the ceiling—about her sleep (poor) and the quiet in the house at night. To show how frightening the nocturnal quiet is, she shrivels up in her chair and holds her shrinking face in both hands. "As long as you listen inside yourself, receiving messages from earlier incarnations," she whispers, "then everything is alright. But if you tune in to the world around you, the smallest sound can terrify you. You're startled by a wardrobe creaking. A fly buzzes behind the stove and you think you're hearing distant voices. The mouse in the attic above you becomes a monster. Downstairs a door squeaks so softly you think it's just your imagination. But isn't that someone coming up the stairs? You don't hear footsteps, just groaning floorboards. The sound comes closer, dreadfully close, then goes away again and heads upstairs. The attic door is jammed, it's always jammed, it's impossible to open without making noise. Then, for hours on end, all you hear is the murmur in your ear. How is a person supposed to sleep when you can't help picturing what's going on up there?"

To give him a feel for her nightly wait, her listener is made to wait right now. Despite the gusts of wind outside, Max's hammering down in the garage, and the vinyl record that has reached its end, thumping away on the rotating turntable, Viktor is pretty sure he can sense the silence. His expectations are great. He's hoping to hear Frau Erika's pillow fantasies. But these she doesn't share with him.

She draws herself up, inhaling deeply, and smooths the nighttime thoughts from her forehead. "I'm fond of the girl," she says, "which is why I don't like seeing her throw herself away like that. The Elephant isn't the one for her." She tends to the record player. The Count of Luxembourg is allowed to sing his heart out now, but only at low volume, because Frau Erika intends to speak her mind. Her lecture is aimed at Sebastian but only actually mentions him in passing. The words *thought, consciousness, spirit, soul, will*, and *disposition* occur most frequently, but all add up to the same thing, namely, energy or formative power. The latter has an amazing influence on the human body, which Frau Erika nicely describes as the soul's garment. Viktor has to admit (which he promptly does by wagging his head) that thoughts impress themselves on a person's face and that the body's gestures, bearing, and condition are all dependent upon a person's inner disposition. Many illnesses are psychological in origin. A person who wants to become sick, will. And it's well known that, under certain circumstances, even death will bow to the human will. In other

50

words, the spirit, though invisible like electricity, is just as real, the proof lies in its effects. Like everything that exists in reality, the spirit is constantly developing. Millions of years have shaped, augmented, and refined it, making it the master of material. It is now in the process (which no one used to believe) of altering our planet. It's also capable (which few believe even today) of shaping ourselves, according to our will—the will just has to be strong enough. Karl Marx was well aware, says Frau Erika, to Viktor's considerable amazement, that theory, that is to say, thought, becomes material force when its quantity increases. That means that every wish brings us one step closer to the object of our desire. An intensity of wishing is conceivable that would guarantee the gratification of our desires. The will can move more than muscles; it can maintain health and could someday even prevent us from dying. The fact that all humans have died up till now doesn't disprove it, because they all *believed* they had to die. They died out of habit, out of resignation. A person who is resigned will inevitably fail in whatever he undertakes. Only the human who is convinced of his immortality from birth on will be given it. The time will come. Progress is unstoppable. The emancipation of the soul is marching forward, at lightning speed. True, a person living today has only limited access to it. That's why it's important to focus your efforts on this limited range of possibilities; whatever you do, do it with all your soul. A person who can put on lipstick or eat asparagus with no other thought in mind is already on the path to happiness. She, Frau Erika, has focused in particular on not letting her capacity for sexual experience be diminished, and sure enough her concentrated will has materialized. Apart from working on herself, it is essential to eliminate harmful influences. Because your inner reservoir has to be filled from outside as well. The filth of doubt and resignation clogs your spiritual plumbing. For that reason Frau Erika has always made sure that she's surrounded by people who are lighthearted, optimistic, loving, and affirmative, especially young people, but only those who are capable of giving and receiving. Because some young people are senile in spirit. This Sebastian, Frau Erika is sorry to say (finally reaching the end of her talk), is one of them. Instead of enriching others spiritually, he poisons them with his nagging, grumbling, and

51

skepticism. He's one of those people who don't hope for happiness and never find it either, he'll never be a success in life because his soul doesn't cry out for it. Frau Erika is not surprised in the least that he's failed in both career and marriage. That he pretends to loathe the unattainable, this she can understand. What she can't accept is that he spreads his germs of unhappiness instead of going into quarantine. Because the negative, vile sphere that surrounds him is infectious.

Finished with her lecture, Frau Erika looks at Viktor invitingly. He feels compelled to show her that the lesson hasn't been wasted on him. "Well, if that's the case," he exclaims, noticing his own hand begin to move while speaking, "the girl will have to be protected from soul poisoning."

A Letter, Unfinished

Viktor is sitting at his typewriter sooner than he expected (and sooner than he wanted). It's afternoon. His room is warmer than the day before because the stove has been stoked more vigorously and the lower pane of the window is draped with a blanket. The window ledge outside has been cleared of snow, the frost flowers on the glass wiped clean. Viktor can sit at the typewriter without freezing. From behind his desk he can look out the window. Beyond the field of snow (called the Back Bush) stand woods dark and gloomy. The treetops blow in the wind. Clouds scud along above them. The clouds sometimes tear open, revealing flecks of blue in the sky. A flock of crows rises up, drifting and whirling in the wind, before dipping behind the trees again.

Viktor thinks, long and hard. At last he commits the first words to paper: Viktor Kösling. He's working on the title page. Neatly typed and lying before him, he hopes it will stimulate his desire to work. He desperately needs it (as a substitute for the compulsion he's used to back home). He can't even remember the full title. It's written down on a piece of paper between the covers of one of his binders, meaning he would have to get up to look for it. He stays seated instead, wanting first to find out if you can see the graveyard from his spot at the window. It's tucked away in the pinewood but should be easy to make out by the bare limbs of its deciduous trees.

The crows rise up again, and Viktor feels compelled to count them. They are only visible for a fleeting moment, so he doesn't succeed. He waits for the next round to try and estimate their number. For a few brief seconds the clouds permit the sun to shine through. The Back Bush begins to sparkle then dies. A dark-gray cloud appears above the woods then passes. The sun and birds now come out simultaneously. The sound of the wind swells up and dies down, fading away altogether. The pinewood stands rigid, yet the clouds scamper on. There's no end to the excitement. Viktor sits like this for ages, enjoying the performance—until he's called to the telephone.

The conversation with his mother is brief; she's got visitors from the equator waiting. Apart from the weather (still threatening), the state of the roads, and Viktor's health, there's the inevitable question about his work, to which he answers, "I have no choice but to be happy." Only one piece of news is pressing, and she can't help but share it: J.K., whom she's talked to long-distance on a daily basis ever since he fell ill, has yet to receive the letter Viktor is expected to write him once a month. He said a New Year's card won't do. "The best thing would be—" says Agnola, before being interrupted by Viktor: "Okay, okay, I'll get right to it."

Back at his desk, he takes the unfinished title page out of the typewriter and inserts a blank sheet. He addresses the well-known man as Papa and suddenly finds he has quite a bit to say about his dissertation: what an important contribution it'll be making to the Marxist-Leninist reassessment of Prussian history, how big the gap is it'll help to close, and how surprisingly relevant it is to the present. It's smooth sailing, with sentences containing words like *legacy, milestone, link in the chain, forces of reaction,* and *tradition.* Then, on the second page, he gets stuck. Convention calls for a few words about his personal affairs. His eyes seek the outdoors again. He's on the lookout for flocks of crows, which are nowhere to be seen.

It's hard for Viktor to write to his father about personal things. He would rather talk in person, because their conversations (which just like the letters he's ordered to write are also divided into two parts) only require Viktor to give an answer. Which is easy enough, since his father (out of habit) only asks the kinds of questions that presuppose the answers he wants to hear. He's not the least bit interested (even if he thinks he is) in knowing what his son is actually thinking, feeling,

54

or experiencing; his only real concern is to ensure that his son is just like him. As taxing as these talks may be, they're often a pleasure for both of them. Viktor delights in how skillfully he's able to toss back the ball his father plays to him, and his father is gratified to see the effects of his child-rearing efforts.

After the divorce, their conversations took place at home in Potsdam. The separation was amicable, his parents never fail to point out, so his father would often stop by and (in his own words) check up on him. Later they started meeting (less frequently) at his father's new villa on the northern outskirts of Berlin, where the second Frau Kösling would provide a cozy atmosphere with candlelight and homemade cakes. Her name is Emilia but she goes by Emil. Viktor was on a first-name basis with her right off the bat, which admittedly wasn't easy for him. Although she's Viktor's age, her gentle overattentiveness makes her seem older than his nervous and voluble mother. Whenever Viktor comes to visit, she expresses her regret that Agnola turns down her invitations. But Agnola has her reasons for declining: she's afraid the silly little chit will only make her laugh. She makes Viktor give her detailed reports, however, even down to their clothing and furnishings. But Viktor has trouble taking in his surroundings when he has to talk. So he makes things up to please his mother. "Just what I thought!" she exclaims with delight when he places van Gogh's *Sunflowers* over the couch. "It figures!" she says when he has them drinking out of Meissen Blue Onion china. And when Viktor puts Emilia in a woolly vest, she cries, "Stop it! You're cracking me up."

Once the official part of their father-son conversation is over, with its sprinkling of political-ideological content, the personal part begins. It starts with a question about his mother's well-being, which may not be great but thanks to her son and her work is always satisfactory. His father listens with an earnest, even concerned expression: certainly her work gives her life meaning and helps her cope. Then an understanding smile announces the next topic: girls. These, Viktor knows, should occupy an important place in the life of a young man like him, but not too important: enhancing yet not determining, not necessarily without attendant problems and pain, but essentially pleasant.

The man-to-man talks began when Viktor was sixteen, peppered with reminiscences about the swinging days of his father's youth. The Pill was dealt with well before Viktor had any use for it. No sirree, his father was no Puritan. Viktor therefore felt obliged to admit to experiences he'd never had. Since his father was once a seducer, the son became one too (in conversation). Girlfriends older than him became younger. And to make sure his father's repeated slogan, "No premature commitments!" wasn't uttered in vain, he invented intentions to tie the knot, then bravely resisted despite the pain.

He can't talk about things like this though in a letter from his rural retreat. When duty commands the whole individual, the heart is bound to silence. It can't be about pleasure, it has to be about burning the midnight oil. A word of complaint is surely permitted, but it has to convey his determination. Humor is good, especially if it's drastic. Landscape and weather are of little interest, the people around him are at least worth a mention. Taken as a whole (and referred to as "our people"), they're naturally a decent lot, although individual specimens are certainly worthy of ridicule. Frau Erika is an obvious candidate, but the idea is quickly discarded because he can't be sure that the hallowedness of the Schulze-Decker name doesn't extend to her as well. Sebastian seems a better choice: the fallen man who dresses up his defeat in philosophical musings, at once both comic and tragic.

While sunshine and blue skies conquer the clouds outside, Viktor embarks on part two of his letter. I'm sitting here in the back of beyond, so to speak, he writes, but hardly even notice. My mind is filled with Prussians, who fail to discern the signs of their time. When I leave my cell-like room, a rare occurrence, I barely perceive the people around me. Apart from the chambermaid, of whom I seldom get a glimpse, and the director's small children, there is no one here but the old and infirm. In other words, life here is quiet and dull.

At a loss for what to write next, Viktor pauses to reflect. He looks out the window and sees a female figure heading for the woods. He won't be finishing his letter today.

Playing Games

The person Viktor wishes to encounter accidentally is trudging across the Back Bush. Viktor stays on Dead Man's Road. Snow is everywhere, up to his knees. The sun, free of clouds, is hanging right above the trees. Viktor makes a beeline for it. The road forks at the edge of the woods: to the right it rounds a tree-lined hill to the dump, to the left it goes up to the wooded cemetery. Juniper trees, brier bushes, and arborvitae skirt the roadway here. The hillsides are marked by rows of graves under pine trees. The rows are linked by paths, some of which have steps. In a leveled depression sits the mortuary, ugly as a garage. The road winds its way up a moderate slope onto a plateau, where it ends. Planks, boards, rope, and spade are deposited behind a pump, a wooden bench, and a wastebasket: everything a gravedigger needs. The ridge of the hill is a little bit higher. A couple of steps lead up to it.

Viktor spots the footprints he's looking for, along with the person who made them. But the figure, who just climbed up the steps, is visible only as a silhouette against a glowing red background because right behind stands the sun, poised to set and bigger than ever. This is a sight of great significance, he reflects, a solemn moment he plans on remembering, so that he can later say: freezing, with wet feet, I stood in the snow and distinctly saw how you came to me from the sun.

But for now he offers a mannerly greeting, followed, once he reaches the steps, by a few words about the woods and snow and fresh air. He doesn't receive an answer, however. Slow and ponderous, the person walks off, past the graves and toward the hillside, stopping at the last tomb, the biggest one, a sturdy glazed-brick structure enclosed by an iron fence. The woman, too massive to be Thilde, digs a broom out from under the snow with her hands and starts to sweep it off.

Viktor knows now that he'll have to be loud if he wants to be heard. Stepping closer, he bellows his greeting into the lovely winter landscape, along with his comment about the beauty of winter. Tita recognizes him immediately, greets him courteously in return, then adds in rebuke, "Every time of the year is beautiful here, Herr Kösling. I've no reason to go to Thuringia." She points with her broomstick to where Herr Kösling should look to confirm the truth of what she says.

It's not hard for Viktor to agree. He even sounds a note of joy despite the volume this requires. "Who needs Thuringia," he yells, "or even Switzerland, when it's so pretty right here?"

By this gross exaggeration Viktor means the prospect before him. Far away, where the sun is about to sink, the woods converge in murky waves. Meadows and fields, crisscrossed by roads and white with snow, spread before it. Arndtsdorf, with its church and red roofs, is situated right in the middle. From there an avenue leads to the lake, frozen over and covered with snow. Prötz, which is on this side of the lake, is hidden from view behind the tops of the nearby pines. In front of these, however, right below the family vault, stretches a ravine-like hollow that, according to Tita, bears the name May Valley, but soon won't need a name at all because it's disappearing—under trash. A roadway leads up to it from Prötz. Trucks come from far away to dump things no longer needed. Ten to twenty yards are all that's left between the top of the trash heap and the cemetery.

Since Viktor's resolution that morning was only to stay away from shovels, he can grab Tita's broom with an easy conscience. Masonry and paths are soon cleared of snow, and Viktor is filled in on Tita's departed. There are eight in all, only three of which are buried here: her husband and parents. The other five, her brothers and sons, lie in French, Russian, and North African soil; only their names are marked on the gravestones. Viktor counts the names three times, each time coming up with nine. Tita solves the mystery for him: Alwine

Lüderitz, née Richter, whose name is inscribed next to Hans Lüderitz, farmer—that's Tita. Her year of birth is already there, only the year of her death is missing behind the hyphen. When her husband died, she decided to have her name chiseled in along with his. "That way," she says, "it'll be cheaper for Thilde."

Having stowed the broom back behind the tomb, Viktor begins to rejoice again, much to Tita's delight. His fervor is now for the sunset: gorgeous, uncommonly beautiful, just like in a fairy tale, is the way he describes it. Tita doesn't comment but stands there proudly, as though she herself made the colors adorning the sky.

On the way back down, she takes Viktor's arm. She's forgotten her cane—that's the reason for her unsteady gait; with her cane she wouldn't need any assistance, she'd give the boy a run for his money. She boasts about her health. She recently went to the doctor, at Thilde's insistence. "And what do you think he found? Nothing at all, that's what. Frau Lüderitz, he said, someday I'd like to be as healthy as you." No sir, she's got nothing to complain about, everything is ticking right with ol' Tita, except for her head, which doesn't always do what it should anymore. Lately she's been forgetting things: today, for instance, her cane, the one she's used to having with her, yesterday the name of the holiday they just had. The one you need the fir tree for, she said to her granddaughter, before laughing, both of them, at the old lady's silliness.

"Granddaughter?" Viktor inquires, acting astonished. "I thought Hilde, or what's-her-name, is your daughter."

His flattery is a bit too thick this time. Tita eyes him suspiciously. He just saw the year she was born, she says, so he knows that when Thilde was born she was as old as Frau Erika is today. "At that age you can maybe *pretend* you want to when younger men are around," she adds, "but you can forget about having babies."

Viktor laughs at her wisecrack, and Tita is reconciled. She explains to him the name of her granddaughter. Klothilde was her grandmother's grandmother. May Thilde be as good to her own grandchildren one day as Klothilde was to Tita. "How old are you, Herr Kösling?"

"Twenty-nine."

"Thilde is twenty-three."

Tita feels responsible for her. She raised the girl herself, took the place of her mother entirely, even kept the house for her. On the other hand, it's her fault that Thilde has to waste away here in solitude. "She lies through her teeth," says Tita, "to talk me into believing she enjoys being here. The truth is, she's scared for me. She's afraid Max will stick me in a home if she doesn't keep an eye out. But I might end up being a hundred years old, I tell her, and then you'll be too old to marry; go back to the hospital where you did your training and hook yourself a doctor, I say. But she just laughs at the idea."

The first stars are twinkling by the time they reach New Glory. Viktor is still debating whether he should ask to see some family pictures when Tita invites him to coffee. At first he hesitates—he really does have to get to work—but then he agrees after all. In the doorway Tita calls for Thilde, but Thilde isn't there. "Where the dickens is that girl!" Tita grumbles, scouring every room, which doesn't take long because there are only three: a small hallway with a mirror and coat hooks, and two rooms off of it, one behind the other, the first of which, the anteroom, is Thilde's living and bedroom. Even to Viktor, who's virtually blind when it comes to furnishings, it's obvious who the room belongs to, because of its homey feel. Wall unit, sofa bed, coffee table, and armchair are the same ones he has in his Berlin apartment. Tita sees the look in his eyes and, goading him to praise it, says, "All very modern!" Viktor obliges her, finding it all very lovely.

Tita's room looks crammed and cozy by comparison, a very grandmotherly room, or as she herself puts it, "an old lady's parlor." It's the larger of the two rooms but seems smaller because of the profusion of furniture, so much you can barely walk. Viktor has time to take a leisurely look at things while Tita heads across the yard to the kitchen to make the coffee. The walls are lined with a plush sofa (which he's sitting on), a wardrobe, a hutch, a chest of drawers, a sideboard, and a bed. There's also a large table, a wingback chair, a footrest, a nightstand, a sewing table, and sewing machine. Except for the wardrobe, which reaches all the way to the ceiling, every surface of every piece of furniture is covered with junk. Plastic bags stuffed full of wool, silk ribbons, yarn, and patches of every imaginable color are strewn between piles of shoeboxes, cigar boxes, and tobacco tins. Ashtrays are filled with buttons, vases prop up puppets, and everywhere you look there are shells.

Viktor has to restrain himself from rummaging through the boxes, but he does walk around, space permitting, to look at the pictures. They're hanging wherever the wall can be reached. Few of them are framed, most are fastened to the wallpaper with pins. They're not art prints, like the three colorful ones hanging in Thilde's room, but photos of every age and format. Viktor sees ladies, gentlemen, couples, classes, families, babies, and old people, all of whom stare back at the viewer with an earnest to nasty expression. Tita is often among them, easily discernible with her overlong chin—King Thrushbeard even as a young bride with wreath and veil. There are females aplenty, predominantly blond, none, however, that look like a Gypsy.

Tita returns with a giant coffeepot and some Christmas stollen. She doesn't bring Thilde with her. Thilde's busy in the building next door. A training course with thirty-five participants is scheduled for the weekend and there's sweeping, dusting, cleaning, and bed-making to be done. Some cots are needed as well, which the man with the shaggy beard ("What's his name again?") has to haul down from the attic. "That's it, Sebastian. Quite an unpleasant individual, don't you think?"

The coffee, which looks more like weak tea, is excellent in Viktor's appraisal. He avoids giving his opinion on Sebastian, and Tita doesn't press him. She loads his plate up with three slices of stollen and is happy her guest is such a good eater. Unfortunately, she can't join in; her dentures can't handle stollen. Raisins and almond slivers get caught between the upper plate and her gums, chafing her mouth. "You understand?"

"Yes, yes," Viktor hastens to say, but he can't prevent her from taking out her uppers and demonstrating exactly what happens. "You were going to say something about Sebastian," he says, and the diversionary tactic works.

With her teeth in her hand and not in her mouth, Viktor has trouble understanding the first couple of sentences. Only as she reaches for her coffee cup does she notice that something is missing and puts the teeth back in her mouth where they belong. She picks up where she left off, this time comprehensibly: Apart from all that, she can't stand it when the only thing someone can appreciate about the soup is the hair he finds in it—that is, when someone is eternally dissatisfied and always has something to criticize. At the mention of duty he turns up his nose, and if he hears the word *order* he starts seeing red. And then that beard of his! Tita's no fan of facial hair. To her it's like a mask, and anyone who needs one of those has something to hide. Who caused the first war? Wilhelm the Bearded. The second? Adolf Mustache. And when she lost her land the Goatee was in power. No sir, she'd never wish Thilde a man with a beard, and if she had any influence over young Viktor he'd get rid of that tiny little patch of hair disfiguring *his* face. "I don't mean to get political," she says, "I'm just saying. Your father doesn't have any facial hair. I don't see why you can't present yourself with a plain and hairless face too."

Viktor is tempted to make Tita a promise. His mustache means little to him. A certain Anja had requested it, and those who came later had nothing against it. Force of habit has kept it there. He doesn't intend to do Grandma the honor, however, until he knows how her granddaughter feels about it. So he distracts her with the photos: bearded and mustachioed men can be seen on them as well. Does this corroborate Tita's facial-hair theory?

He knows well enough that he's in for the family photos now. What he doesn't realize is the extent of them. The pictures adorning the walls are just the icing on top; the massive cake he'll have to eat his way through is lying about unorganized in boxes big and small.

Tita doesn't make it easy on him, or brief for that matter. She's never content with simple explanations like "That's me in Klein-Kietz," "That's my son Kurt in the army," "The eighth from the left in the third row is Uncle Franz," or the occasional "I'm not sure who that is anymore." She revels in the memories the pictures evoke, turning them into stories that tend to never end. For example, fourteen-year-old Alwine (who later becomes Tita) is standing long-chinned (naturally), in a long skirt and a white apron, pouring a beer from the tap behind the counter of the Good Friend Inn in Klein-Kietz. Her comment, however, runs as follows: "Right next to the counter to the left, right about *there*, that's where the door to the ballroom was, one of those big double doors, and when the fireman's ball, the reservist ball, or some other shindig was going on, Karl was always standing near the door so he could see me, waiting for a break at the bar so he could fetch me for a dance or two, preferably waltzes, which I always liked best, so much that I couldn't stand it when he talked while we were dancing, he was only allowed to sing along: 'It cannot remain so forever, here under the changeable moon.' You don't know that one anymore? Such a lovely song. 'It cannot remain so forever, here under the changeable moon, la la la la la lala la la la, and wither away all too soon.' It was seven or eight verses long, and I knew them all like the back of my hand. I'll have to ask Thilde, she knew them by heart, like me, when she was little. The part she understood best was the line that went: 'dadamdam dadamdam dadam, who knows, then, how soon we'll be scattered, by fate to the East and the West.' Just like what happened to her mother, because a man was involved, obviously."

Faced with a self-perpetuating story like this, the best Viktor can do is grab another picture and toss in a question: "And who's this?" But when he makes the mistake of asking who this Karl guy is standing in the doorway to the ballroom, Tita gets all worked up and says, "The fellow with the hat? We've done him already." She weeds through the cigar box they've already plowed through and, returning to the picture of her at the counter again, is reminded of other things: the brewer's drayman from Küstrin, for example, who, like his lumbering horses, wore a lot of leather and brass, and whenever he saw Alwine liked to say: it shouldn't be called the Good Friend but the Beautiful Girlfriend Inn!

The remarkable thing about Tita's memory is that the further back in time she travels, the bigger her store of memories gets. Whereas her husband and his siblings are never present, and her sons, daughters, and granddaughter seldom, her grandparents, parents, aunts, great aunts, uncles, and brothers figure among her fondest memories, even though she has fewer pictures of them. Little Tita, or rather Alwine, the preschool and school-age child, is more distinct in Tita's mind than Tita the wife, farmer, mother, and grandmother. She can't locate her sons in a class picture from the thirties, but the yellowed photo from her own Klein-Kietz school days inspires her to go off on a myriad of tangents. Of course, Viktor first has to spot her in the picture and is applauded when he recognizes her (he doesn't say what tipped him off). Then she explains to him the teaching methods used in a one-room village schoolhouse. Then he learns the name of her teacher—a man with a stand-up collar and center part—and what happened to him later (killed for the Fatherland), as well as who came before and who came after him. The nineteen pupils in her school are listed by name and their achievement-based seating arrangement elaborated. Hans Opoczynski, that little rascal right there, gave her her first kiss out in the cowshed. Joachime Matthieu, the minister's daughter, later married the mayor of Crossen but died in the first week of child-bed. That fellow there, the one gaping like an idiot, was Tita's cousin, who later inherited the farm and the inn. A loathsome creature, you can tell in this group photo right here: more than twenty people of all ages with eyes wide open, standing and sitting in front of New Glory. There are other Kietzers there apart from the idiotic cousin. They came by carriage, meaning a day there and a day back, but how could they not make the trip when Tita's oldest brother was getting married. There he is, the groom—without his bride. A sturdy girl alright, but afraid to have her picture taken. She was widowed a year later, but only a year of mourning before she married the miller from Hoppschugge, survived him as well, and now lives alone by the deserted and half-dilapidated mill. The girl next to the groom is not the bride in other words, she's the sister-in-law of the sister—no, wait, her name was Auguste and she was the sister of the sister-in-law of Uncle Fritz's wife—no, it was like this . . .

But Viktor never learns how it was, because the dinner bell rings before she can finish. He's back, as promised, for more pictures after dinner, but the sister-in-law or sister of whomever has since been forgotten. With the aid of a postcard of the Good Friend Inn, Tita is now trying to recall the layout of rooms. She gets stuck on the first floor, and Viktor uses the brief intermission to voice a request. He'd like to see a picture of Thilde. Nothing easier, says Tita. All he has to do is get up, pass through the narrow corridor between sewing table and sewing machine, turn to the right at the ironing board, and there it is, hanging between the tiled stove and the wardrobe up against the wall. Lying on a fur rug, naked and with a look of fright on her face, is Thilde, not yet one year old. "How sweet!" is all Viktor can muster up in his disappointment. He returns to his waiting and torture chair.

Tita is happy to have Herr Kösling's company because twenty-three-year-old Thilde will be busy into the evening making up the guest beds with Sebastian. "I'm not boring you, am I?" she asks while fishing out another box of pictures from the chest of drawers. Viktor, fairly overcome by weariness at this point, says, "No, not at all, I'm extremely interested," and, to prove it, asks a question about the very next picture, which will seal his fate for the evening.

The picture shows Tita and her sons sitting around an outdoor table, absorbed in some game. Viktor asks what game they're playing but draws a blank when she tells him. He doesn't know it. And how would he? There were no games at the Kösling home. Tita can't believe it. "What!?" she cries out, "Are you kidding me? Impossible. The best game of all time and you don't know it?" She's played it all her life—with her grandmother, her brothers, her sons, and then her granddaughter. It's a cinch to learn and loads of fun. She's possessed by a missionary zeal, making all resistance futile. You can't just tell a fanatic like her, Sorry, I can't keep my eyes open.

She doesn't even have to stand up to get it, just reaches into the drawer of the table and voilà—a flimsy game board folded in half and patched up with Scotch tape, edges torn and surface partly worn away, painted with lines and colorful circles, and in the middle, written in old German script, the name of the game: Aggravation!

The board is two-sided, one side for six players, the other for four. A twosome can opt for either side but it's better to use the four-player version. Each player gets four of the colorful pieces, called stones. Tita lays claim to yellow, the color she's been used to ever since childhood. She recommends red to Viktor. The colored stones are placed on matching circles in one corner. All they need now is the leather cup with the die. It's in the sideboard. Viktor fetches it and the fun begins. But first things first: the first person to roll a six gets to start.

Tita laughs like a child, grabbing the cup with one hand and holding it shut with the other. After ample shaking, she slams it upside down on the table. The cup still covering the die, she gives her opponent a mischievous grin. Finally she takes a deep breath and removes the cup with a jerk. A six! "Well, there you have it," says Tita, barely able to contain herself. Viktor only rolls a five, so Tita has the honor. "Hoo-wee, I'm on a roll," she says when she gets another six. She moves her first stone and gets to roll again on top of it. This time it's just "a measly one," so it's Viktor's turn to try his luck.

Tita has still other methods of charming the die apart from protracted shaking. She gently tips it out of the cup when hoping for a low number and tosses it clear across the table when she needs a five or six. Symbolically spitting on the die three times will sometimes do the trick. When crunch time comes, however, when the whole game is riding on it, she sets the cup down on the table, places her hands along the rim in the shape of a funnel, puts her mouth up to it, and whispers the desired number three times.

The first game is a practice run. She offers advice and instruction, allowing the novice to correct his mistakes. Once the second game gets under way, the rules are binding and a move is a move, even if it spells disaster. Tita is a shrewd and ruthless player who takes gleeful pleasure in harming her opponent. If the number she rolls enables her to send Viktor's stone back to start, the impending triumph is evident in her tone of voice: "A five!" she crows, "Well, isn't that just lovely," and she counts out her move with sublime slowness, the pitch steadily rising to four, then dropping at five, the fatal blow. Viktor does her the favor of looking unhappy. "Don't be aggravated now!" she says, her face lit up with joy.

Tita never tires of playing. She confesses that once she gets started she forgets about everything, even sleep. At first Viktor is infected by her enthusiasm, but by ten o'clock his fervor has subsided. It is then that the door opens just a crack and Thilde announces her return. She's had her bath already and is going to bed now but don't mind her, they can go on playing. Tita, in the midst of rolling a string of sixes, has just enough time to declare that she's won five times already. Then the door closes, without Viktor so much as getting a glimpse. He now insists they wrap things up.

They end up playing three last games, the final one at midnight, and even then Viktor is only allowed to go after promising he'll come back tomorrow at the first opportunity. The light stays out as he passes through Thilde's room on his tiptoes. Viktor can hear the sleeping girl's breathing. Its rhythm haunts him all the way to bed. Drifting to sleep, he tries to harmonize his own breathing with hers.

The unfinished letter to his father doesn't cross his mind until the next day. And only then does he notice the envelope on his desk, embellished with roses and addressed to His Royal Highness Prince Hamlet of Denmark, on the premises.

The Advantages of Heating by Stove

Up until now Viktor hasn't given much thought to the man-high tiled stove in his room. Not so the following morning. Now he gazes at it dreamily, strokes its brown tiles, and occasionally (if it's not too hot) puts his cheek up against it.

Viktor grew up in apartments where the necessary heat doesn't have to be generated but is there for the taking—like electricity and gas. He never actually knew what was being burned where or by whom. His dissatisfaction with the temperature of a room was similar to his feelings about the weather. A defective boiler at the heating plant couldn't have been more remote, and impervious to his influence, than a polar low. This explains why it takes so long for him to realize that the comfortable temperature of his individual room requires an individual to stoke the fire.

It was Tita who prompted this realization by discussing the work of the chambermaid. Viktor lingered on the thought, imagined the girl dusting and sweeping, making beds, and, ultimately, firing up the stove. And thus the plan was born that he intends to carry out on the morning of his fourth day at New Glory.

He's only ever experienced the stove as warm; he's never actually seen a fire being made in it. They must wait, he muses, until he leaves the room before setting to work lighting the fire. And so as not to have to constantly keep an eye on him, they must do it during meal-times. This is the key to his plan.

He places a fresh handkerchief on the nightstand in plain view. Whistling loudly, he heads downstairs, crosses the yard, and enters the dining room. Köpke is just being served his second cup of coffee, to complement his morning cigar. Each day he comes to breakfast as early as possible in order to enjoy it alone. He neither feels nor feigns the slightest pleasure as Olga takes Viktor's order with a show of hospitality. Viktor's hearty good-morning greeting only succeeds in extracting a nod from him. It's obvious he's itching to take his cup and sit down at another table. Viktor is tortured. Unable to busy him-self with breakfast because he doesn't have any yet, he tries to strike up a conversation by asking how the deer fare in cold weather, but the hunter says only, "Very well, thanks!" and looks right past him. The moment has come, thinks Viktor, to mention the cold he's afraid he's coming down with. He checks his pants pockets and notes that he doesn't have a handkerchief on him. "I'll be right back," he says to Köpke, in a consoling tone, and rushes out the door, only to be held up in the yard. "Hey, Kösling, over here!" the gardener calls out. He's standing at the gate with Max and Manuela. Viktor covers his ears with his hands while walking, which is meant to signify: I'm not hang-ing around for long, it's cold out here.

He's arrived just in time for a joyous occasion. Griepenkerl, so he hears (a name with which neither he nor the reader is familiar), has done it; just another hundred yards and he'll be there. You can hear him in the yard already. Viktor can even see him from the gate: a trac-tor with a snowplow, big, red, and noisy. Connection to the outside world has been reestablished.

Griepenkerl's fat face beams with delight when he sees how happy the others are. He climbs down from the quivering beast like a conqueror. Viktor's hand hurts from Griepenkerl's handshake. Max has brought schnapps and cigarettes. Viktor has to take a swig at Se-bastian's insistence. The gardener calls him by his first name. That must hark back to their evening of grog and conversation, only parts of which have been preserved in Viktor's memory. When Manuela leaves the group, bored by their talk of snow and machinery, Viktor points out his freezing hands and ears and follows her. You can tell by her walk that she knows the person behind her is enjoying the view. "No school today?" Viktor asks, feeling somewhat perky from the alcohol. A nasty look and a "Phh!" are all he gets for an answer.

He hurries up the steps then slows his pace. The door to his room is ajar, a broom and several buckets next to it. His assumption, then, was right. The encounter he's been hoping for is just around the corner. But he isn't prepared, he hasn't studied his part. This is unusual; while he can react spontaneously to others, he's not very good at conducting conversations on his own. He's only planned up to the moment he sees her face and is now afraid he'll just stare at her admiringly without being able to utter a word.

The thought is negated before he can even finish thinking it, however. No sooner is the face before him than he comes up with the right words after all. He knows them only when he hears them. A voice issues from inside him, and not the worst one either, he later concludes. This is a totally new experience. It occurs to him in the evening that things are more serious than ever before.

The act he's putting on without so much as a second thought, and with considerable success, is that of exposure, of laying himself bare, the charm of sincerity, touching, bewildering, and comical at once. He plays a Viktor who commands the usual diversion tactics but nevertheless despises them, who is perfectly capable of being like everyone else but who prefers to let his individuality shine through instead. He could surely hide his interest in Thilde, as a matter of decorum, but he's too good for that, recognizing at first blush that deception isn't needed here, that he's free to be the person he is.

Thus, he opens the door and is startled to find there someone he's disturbing, apologizes, says hello, mutters a pathetic lie about an oncoming cold, reaches for the handkerchief he accidentally forgot on purpose, brings it to his nose and blows, does so again and laughs while snorting, quietly, but loud enough to be heard. It's obvious he doesn't want to laugh, but he can't help it. He excuses himself, still laughing. He's not laughing at her, he's laughing at himself—at the act he's putting on here, which she obviously sees through, judging by the smile he sees on her face. It wasn't the sniffles but curiosity which lured him back from the breakfast table. It would be ridiculous to try and hide it. He has been here four days already and still hasn't gotten a glimpse of the solicitous soul that heats his room for him, makes his bed, and sweeps the snow off his window ledge. His curiosity is therefore excusable, particularly when it is mixed with a bad conscience and gratitude. Because he's perfectly capable of making his own bed in the morning, and because he's come to appreciate the blanket in the window to keep out the draft while working at his desk—that is, when he isn't distracted, as he often is, by wondering what the girl looks like who makes sure his feet are warm. He makes no bones about his having made some initial inquiries. He's even seen a picture of her: as a baby on a bearskin rug. It is certainly understandable that, rather than satisfying his curiosity, this only piqued it.

He says all this lightheartedly, and Thilde takes it just as lightly. Her question, "I suppose you're disappointed now?" is more jesting than flirtatious. Viktor shakes his head vigorously, cries out, "Not at all, far from it!" so loudly that his enthusiasm borders on the comical, then resumes his confession: he never saw the whole of her face, but the parts he saw, he saw correctly, so that, seeing it now for the first time in full, her face seems quite familiar, actually. He doesn't know if Fräulein Thilde has heard Frau Erika's theory of reincarnation, but if so, she'll understand what he means when he says he feels like he knew her in a previous life. Not that he believes in that kind of stuff, he's just mentioning it to help explain the feeling he has, a distant feeling from the deepest depths and which the word *familiarity* only captures in the most superficial sense. It means more than just "not foreign," it means close, congenial, and confidence-inspiring, like kindred spirits. He's never experienced anything like it before: he sees somebody for the first time and right away there's this awesome sense of trust. He could confess to her right here, on the spot, about everything that's been burdening his soul.

Viktor is so enthusiastic talking about Thilde's face that it's not quite clear whether he isn't just saying it for the sake of comic relief.

There is therefore no cause for awkwardness between them. She can laugh at him the way he laughs at himself—and she laughingly advises him to have a hearty breakfast before confession.

He's taken a seat on the bed so as not to be looking down at her. Thilde is kneeling in front of the stove, unperturbed in her work. The kindling is already crackling. She heaps the coal into the stove from a bucket. The glow of the fire illuminates her face. Viktor is able to study it closely while putting on his little farce. He sees (but doesn't say) that her mouth really is too big, and that her forehead, absent from his recollections, is hidden from view once again, being covered all the way down to her thick eyebrows by bangs. Viktor wishes the bangs weren't there, since they shorten and darken her face.

Thilde is just closing the upper door of the stove and turning the knob when she makes her funny remark about breakfast. She stands up and grabs the broom. Viktor is clever enough not to spoil the good impression he's made by hanging around too long. He takes a deep bow at the door, saying, "It was a pleasure for me."

"For me, too," says Thilde, adding her hope that his head cold goes away.

Their conversation does not last long. Griepenkerl is still standing at the gate with Max and Sebastian. Köpke puts out his cigar and decamps, so there's no need for Viktor to make a show of his handkerchief the way he planned to. His egg and coffee are cold but in no danger of spoiling his good mood. He feels like being friendly to everyone. Tita is the first to profit from his urge. When she sticks her head through the kitchen doorway and invites him over for the afternoon, he confirms it with such a shout that she shakes her head and rebukes him: "You don't have to talk any louder to me than to the others, Herr Kösling. Just a little more clearly than people are wont to these days."

HARMONY OF SOULS

More richly adorned than the envelope itself—addressed to Prince Hamlet, on the premises—is the letter inside. Garlands of roses, bunched together in the corners, frame an exceedingly neat, sometimes frilly handwriting, inscribed on the paper with a fine-tipped pen, black on pale pink stationery. There are eight sheets in all, each of them written on one side. Certain words have been underlined with a ruler in light blue (a color not used for the roses). Viktor marvels at the sight. Standing at his desk, he first reads the salutation ("My prince!"), followed by the ending ("Eagerly awaiting your reply. Love, Fairy"), then sitting down with furrowed brow, the whole thing, which is not quite as voluminous as the amount of paper she used would suggest:

Night. Silence all around. The fireplace quietly hums. People and animals are fast asleep. My own little bed beckons to slumber, yet sleep eludes me. I'm pondering the hope that came and went today, leaving me conflicted. (New paragraph.) A prince came to my humble quarters—strong yet gentle—both manly and innocent—a glint of heaven seemed to shimmer around him. He held out his arms to me—four hands met of their own accord—radiant glances flowed into one another—hidden currents ebbed and flowed—an inner ferment raged and subsided—a miracle had occurred: kindred souls had found each other without words! (New paragraph.) Oh, what are words!? An empty ringing to those who know the soul's true language. (New paragraph.) There where harmonies ring in their souls, the soul's garment longs to whirl in sync eternally. Happiness in mortal (underlined in light blue) flesh can be born of spiritual community, the beauteous kind. So I thought, so I sang, yet fate, alas, had other plans. The prince's heart, I seem to hear, is beating a different rhythm. His mind is set on another goal. The hand clasped fraternally in mine wishes to hold the hand of another. The currents of desire seek other regions. I take to tranquil shores. Adieu, my hope, I bid thee farewell! (New paragraph.) Believe me, my prince: the only happiness which doesn't contain a seed of disappointment sure to sprout the moment we encounter it is the happiness of dreams. (New paragraph.) A fairy-tale dream, a dream of a fairy tale. Once upon a time there was a prince who was banished to a distant castle. The castle stood in a region dark and lonely, and dark and lonely was the prince's heart. One day, while strolling sadly through the corridors of the castle, he chanced upon a maiden there. He greeted her, she returned his greeting, but when he tried to speak she ran away in fear. So he sent out his servants to observe her, and from them he learned: 'twas a handmaid with a bridegroom, and the bridegroom was a menial. Now, in the castle lived since time immemorial a fairy. The fairy had had her fair share of experience, yet, as is the wont of fairies, hadn't grown old in the process. Her heart was particularly young. When she saw the prince her heart came ablaze. One day she contrived to lure the prince into her chamber. Seeing that he was sad, she said, "Don't be sad, prince, my heart is ablaze, and if it shall please you, come o' nights to put it out." Yet the prince wept disconsolately, and when she pressed him he spoke: "I'm weeping because love only brings each one of us suffering; the fairy suffers because she loves the prince, the prince suffers because he loves the handmaid, and things aren't so rosy with the handmaid and the menial either, the menial not being worthy of her love." At this point the fairy began weeping with him. She wept and wept till her tears washed away all the selfishness from her love. Then, when her soul was as clear as a spring, she said to the prince: "Weep no longer, prince, everything will turn out well." Shortly thereafter, the fairy paid a visit to the handmaid. She won her trust and, without the handmaid so much as noticing, poured her love for the prince into her. Ere long the prince and the handmaid became a happy couple. The only unhappy person was the menial. The fairy, as a reward for her beneficence, was allowed to share in the happiness she had sown. Hence, whenever the prince and the handmaid extinguished the fire in their hearts, the fairy was with them in her dreams. Anyone who's experienced life like the teller of this tale has will envy the fairy for the constancy and purity of her happiness. (New paragraph.) Prince! I propose to you a pact, not with the Devil but with a fairy. I will do everything in my power to help you achieve your goal, whereas you, for your part, will help me dream! My lips have touched this letter (big paragraph break) right here. Press your lips to the very same spot and the pact is sealed. (New paragraph.) The roses' eternal splendor on these pages is commensurate to an ever unfulfilled desire. Reality soon wilts, on which one's spent his powers: true paradise it seems, on paper truly flowers! (New paragraph.) Good night, prince, sleep well! Eagerly awaiting your reply. Love, Fairy.

Having read this peculiar letter, Viktor now understands the meaning of "mixed feelings." The mix is so faultless he really can't pin down just what he is feeling at all. He's amused, of course, but frightened as well; he's aroused in both a pleasant and an unpleasant way. He's compassionate and scornful at the same time, repulsed, moved, and flattered. He's just as prepared to flee from the attack as he is to hold his ground with honor. There's also an element of calculation, probing the extent of Frau Erika's leverage, along with the triumph of again having managed to please someone. The pleasure he derives gives rise to gratitude, which obliges him, in turn, to write back. Just thinking about it inclines him to adopt Frau Erika's style, he searches for words and expressions that might appeal to her. The task is alluring. He pushes the typewriter aside and sets a piece of stationery down in front of him, regretfully not the colored kind. He goes back to the big paragraph break in Frau Erika's letter and (sensing the urge to look over his shoulder) actually presses his lips to the paper. Amazingly, he finds it stimulating, as if he really did just kiss someone, a thirty-years-younger Frau Erika perhaps. That's the way he has to picture her if he wants his letter to be warm and affectionate. Yet he also wants to remain detached, without being impolite, because he's not quite sure just what her plans are. His guardedness is such that he's afraid to use the word "I." Involuntarily, his handwriting becomes bolder and more sweeping than usual. His capital letters are suddenly adorned with flourishes. It pleases him that his writing looks foreign. He doesn't end up writing much, but it takes him a very long time to do so, particularly because of the rhymes, which are hard for him to find. He tries to think of poems he learned in school, in order to find the right rhythm, but all that comes to mind is "Risen from the Ruins" and "Brothers, Towards Sun, Towards Freedom."

It takes him until four in the afternoon to finish. He addresses the envelope "Fairy Godmother, on the premises." On his way to Tita's room, he knocks on Frau Erika's door. "Special delivery! A letter, for you!" he says as she opens the door. By the look on her face, you'd think he were the mailman. She thanks him with friendly indifference and closes the door. Then she reads:

Dear Fairy Godmother, A gloomy morning. Outside nothing but gray clouds, cold and deathly white. Inside not a spark of hope or joyfulness. Work, whose shadow darkens the senses of the sleeping, blackens the day with unrelenting compulsion. But then his gaze alights upon a letter. A sweet bouquet doth bloom, where e'er the eye reposes, brings light to gravelike gloom. Thanks to thee, fay of roses! (New paragraph.) The fairy, it seems, is endowed with supernatural powers. Like a book she reads the prince's heart. There's nothing she doesn't see. He could feel ashamed at being seen through, yet, oh! wonder of wonders, not shame is what the prince discovers upon peering into his deepest soul but joy at having found a confidante of his expectations. (New paragraph.) No longer are they lonely; tied by mutual devotion, fairy and prince set off, hand in hand, in search of bliss and happiness. (New paragraph.) The pact is made, two pairs of lips have sealed it. The fairy's dream and the prince's reality can now begin. Yet where does the path to happiness lie? Love, Prince.

Peppermint Liqueur

Viktor has resolved to be firm with Tita this afternoon because, after all, he has work to do. "Three games, tops!" is his resolution, and he means it too—that is, unless certain younger relatives happen to show up.

But Tita is alone and, what's more, completely changed. She's fidgety and depressed and has forgotten all about their rendezvous. Her question, "What can I do for you?" embarrasses him. He virtually has to force her to play, feigning cheerfulness to cheer her up. He imitates her magic formulas when rolling and laughs out loud when they fail to help him. But Tita doesn't pay any attention to him. He keeps having to remind her to roll. She counts incorrectly, moves the wrong pieces, and occasionally forgets about the game entirely. It occurs to her that she needs her walking stick, but getting up to go fetch it, she doesn't remember why she stood up. She sits back down in her chair stiffly and closes her eyes; stroking her chin with rapid hand movements, she's suddenly startled, then accuses Viktor of cheating. She uses the familiar mode of address.

She's aggravated at losing the first game but no longer notices when she loses the second. She gets up hurriedly and wanders around the room, rubbing her hands as if in despair. She hears but doesn't answer Viktor's questions, responding instead with meaningless pleasantries. She says, "With pleasure," "Whatever you say," "Very kind of you," yet stands at the window wringing her hands. Then she wanders between the junk-covered furniture again. Fear is in her eyes. Her lips are constantly moving, as though softly reciting prayers. Absent a will of her own, she lets herself be escorted to the sofa and sits down, but jumps to her feet again as soon as Viktor releases her arm. "Should I go get Thilde?" he yells in her ear. "Very thoughtful," she says, not comprehending.

In the hallway, he runs into the newly arrived training-course participants, who address him as Comrade Director. He refers them to Max, who for once is using the office to receive his weekend visitors (together with Püppi). Max informs him that Thilde is firing up the stoves in the rooms above the dining hall. He thus finds her in front of a stove again. Firelight flickers across her face again, her forehead covered by bangs. And again he's impressed by her mouth, which he still finds rather large but not overly so. It seems appropriate that after their initial, lighthearted encounter they should meet this time on a more solemn note, since they're now on different terms. He doesn't hide his concern about Tita. What he does hold back is the pleasure he derives from displaying how concerned he is. He appears so frightened by the state Tita's in that Thilde feels compelled to comfort him: she's seen it before and knows it will pass. They still have to hurry, though, because Viktor left the door to her room unlocked. He should always lock it, she tells him as they cross the yard, when Tita's in a state like this. Viktor is delighted at hearing the word *always* because of the permanency it suggests and is eager to confirm that yes, in future he'll always be sure to lock the door, this he promises.

The hallway is full of luggage. More gentlemen in city clothes have arrived and are standing in line outside the office. Püppi screams when one of them attempts a funny face. Gabi and Thomas are standing by to escort them to their rooms. A jovial fellow with a full beard sighs with inflated admiration—Aah!—as Thilde walks past.

Thilde heaves a sigh of relief when she sees that Tita's still there. Viktor follows suit. He watches attentively the way Thilde handles her grandmother, affectionate yet stern. "What's the matter now?" she asks, stroking Tita's hair. "There's no reason to be upset." She takes Tita's arm, walks around with her, talking nonstop, then seats her on the sofa. "C'mon, speak up. What's wrong? Why are you making such a fuss?"

Much to Viktor's surprise, Tita wears a guilty expression. She turns and looks the other way, like a naughty child who feels remorse but isn't willing to show it. Thilde forces Tita to look at her and answer her questions. "It was just . . . ," Tita says in a whining voice, unable to finish her sentence because of her tearless sobs. "It was just . . ."

"What was it?"

"It was just that a strange man was in my room all of a sudden."

"You don't say," says Thilde. "It was just Herr Kösling, you know. You asked him to come. He was just trying to be friendly and wanted to play a game or two. And you had to go and scare him off. He's probably had enough of you now."

"Don't be ridiculous," Viktor interjects, wanting to elaborate. But Thilde looks at him and shakes her head, indicating that he should just keep quiet so as not to disturb her corrective measures, which apart from more admonishments also involve some blandishments. She has three more stoves to tend to, then she's free for a while. If Tita stays calm and doesn't do anything silly, they might just be able to play a little game afterward, maybe even (with an inquiring look at Viktor, who is nodding vigorously) a threesome. It will take her about half an hour to finish with the stoves. She'll turn on the television in the meantime to dispel any foolish thoughts.

It's not clear whether Tita has understood. She willingly lets herself be ushered into Thilde's room and shown to an armchair. Tropical fish glide across the screen, moving their fins to the rhythm of the music. Tita stares at the set obediently. Viktor sits down too, as though it were only natural for him to stay. "You don't have to," says Thilde softly, "I can lock the door."

"I don't have to," answers Viktor, "but it's better this way."

Waddling penguins march over a cliff. Tita quickly gets up from her chair. She walks to the door, opens it a crack, and watches Thilde leave. "She's gone," Tita whispers to Viktor. "Now's our chance, let's make it snappy! We have to get out of here, fast! Where's my cane?" She hurries to her room, starts searching behind cabinets, under tables, tearing open drawers. Viktor follows her around, trying to reason with her. Even when he adopts Thilde's tone of voice—"Hey, what's the big idea here!"—his words have no effect.

"Shut your trap!" she snaps right back at him. "Doggone it, where's my cane?"

Viktor decides to change tactics. While Tita is rummaging around making a racket, Viktor goes to Thilde's room and locks the door to the hallway. He sticks the key into his jacket. Then he helps her look. Her cane is under the bed. He kicks it well out of reach, all the way to the wall. Tita finds her summer coat while foraging through the wardrobe. She slips it on and ties a scarf around her head. "C'mon," she says, "we have to hurry!" Viktor reminds her of the cane, and she renews her search, this time behind the laundry pile on top of the chest of drawers. "Well, looky here," she says all of a sudden, "just look what I have here." She waves a half-full bottle cheerfully. "Medicine," she says and laughs out loud. She opens the bottle and puts it to her mouth, but Viktor cries out, "No, don't, there are glasses for that!"

This time she obeys him. She sits down at the table, Viktor brings the glasses, and Tita pours. "Cheers! To medicine!" After the second glass, the sweet green liqueur begins to take effect. Viktor inquires with a laugh how the medicine got behind the laundry pile, and Tita explains with a laugh of her own that that's her little secret. Clinking glasses a fourth time, they're suddenly startled by a knock at the door. Viktor can't find the key right away and has to laugh again as the knock becomes a hammer.

By the time he returns to the room with Thilde, bottle and glasses have magically disappeared. Tita is sitting crumpled up on the sofa, her head on the armrest. Thilde leans over her solicitously and asks what's wrong, but her grandma just sits there looking sick, without so much as a word. Granddaughter looks at Viktor quizzically. Viktor has since taken a seat, just to be on the safe side, his legs having begun to show signs of weakness. "There's no reason to be alarmed," he says, doing his best to stifle his laughter. "Nothing bad has happened, she's just a little tipsy."

He doesn't understand why Thilde is so upset by the bottle. Not wanting to add to her sadness, he doesn't say a word about Tita's escape plans—but has plenty of words to spare while making his departure (a successful one, he later assures himself). He holds Thilde's hand longer than necessary. "Please," he says, "there's no reason to thank me.

You're much more worthy of thanks than I am, I'll tell you why some other time. You have to get Tita to bed now, and I have to get to work. Let's just hope that Tita's derangement—I have to admit, it scared me—let's just hope it's over by tomorrow. If it isn't, or if a similar occurrence ever takes place—and I'm afraid it could—just know that you can always count on me, day or night. It's not a bother, believe me. It's a pleasure. I haven't known her for long but I have to admit, I've really become attached to your grandmother. I never had one of my own, but often dreamed of having one."

His powers of concentration just barely suffice to string together this measured and careful explanation. Exhausted and woozy from all the alcohol, he drags himself up to his room and sleeps, briefly but soundly. Late evening finds him wide-awake.

Work and Love, from a
Dialectic Perspective

Viktor's feelings toward his dissertation have undergone a change. The alarming thing about it is that rather than being alarmed he's relieved by the change, having come to the realization that other things are more important to him right now than work. Inspired by alcohol (this time beer), he comments on it later that evening during a conversation: "You never manage to do everything you want or should. If all that counts for you is work, your work will end up dragging you down—that and a bad conscience on top of it. This is not good. You'll die of suffocation, and if you're dead, you won't get anything done. If you succeed, however, in detaching yourself from your work, you'll be able to live pressure-free, in other words you'll be healthy. And then, who knows, you might just get your work done."

The person he says this to is called Matthias, Matthi for short, a broad-shouldered blond with bad skin who arrived at New Glory on Friday afternoon, is leaving on Sunday evening, and is busy in the meantime lecturing, eating, sleeping, and guzzling beer—the latter together with Viktor. Matthi studied political science and worked for two years in Viktor's department before returning to academia, where they're happy to have such a young and aspiring cadre member. Matthi is ambitious as can be. It was Matthi's example that Viktor measured himself against back then, recognizing his own deficiency in this area, which he naturally took pains to disguise. And now all of a sudden he dares, in front of this marvel of a man, to extol his detachment from his work! What strange change, he asks himself while pontificating, has meanwhile taken place in him? Was he that susceptible to the gardener's lecture out in the snowdrifts? Is it the neutral surroundings? Has he gained self-confidence?

Repeating his new discovery in different words (not to be like Olga, but to get an astonished Matthias to open his mouth), he still can't get over it himself. Even more amazing, though, is that Matthi, this shining example of assiduousness, doesn't gainsay him; he agrees with Viktor's assertion, if only with respect to the one who's preaching it. "You can afford it," is Matthi's response.

Among the virtues comprising Matthi's work ethic—and that make dealing with him so disagreeable—is a frankness that despises politeness as duplicity and metes out friendliness according to merit. Thus, the tone he uses when talking to Viktor is peevish rather than amiable. Viktor tries to take the edge off it by drinking to Matthi and changing the subject to gallstones, which, Viktor knows, have been troubling his former colleague. They dip their lips in foam, filling their bellies with diluted malt beverage, talk about illnesses, and later, thanks to the doggedness of one of them, come back to their earlier topic: what the budding Dr. Viktor can afford and Dr. Matthi, who'll soon be a professor, can't. Why is this so? For the simple reason that one of them has Kösling as a father, the other a finance clerk in the District Council of Greiz. If you're already at the top, says Matthi with foam (beer foam) on his mouth, you don't need to be hardworking and full of energy to work your way up. He thinks it's preposterous that Kösling's son would boast about his lack of ambition. He, Matthias, could be every bit as proud of not wanting to learn how to speak in a Saxon dialect.

Matthi is all wrought up. He picks a pimple on his nose, sees the blood, dabs at it carefully, and utters something in Latin. Viktor doesn't follow, is promptly given a translation, and finds it odd to be compared with Jupiter. "And what, may I ask, is an ox like you denied that Jupiter is allowed?"

"Being lazy, for example," Matthias answers.

Viktor has had enough—of this kind of talk and of beer. He wants to go to bed and reminisce about the day's events. He stands up but doesn't dare walk away while the other is still talking to him. So he continues listening to Matthi's reinterpretation of the wisdom of antiquity. Didn't Viktor say that life is more important than work? When Matthi hears the word *life*, he's inclined to inquire if it's blond or brunette. Nothing against love, he adds—it's just that it's not as selfless as it pretends to be. It tends to grow better not in poor and sandy soil, but in rich and fertile ground—which some people are born with under their feet and others have to work like an ox to acquire. That's the difference he's talking about. The question of love or work only applies to a certain person and not to another: for the other, love has to be earned through work. He, for example—university instructor Matthias—knows this all too well. Long enough did he suffer the pangs of rejection; having had the chance to develop his skills in the lecture hall, however, he's literally spoiled for choice. The dialectics of love and work, he calls it, slurring his speech, before popping open another bottle.

Viktor takes the opportunity to leave. Back in his room, another pink letter awaits him. He tears it open and the mixture of joy and aversion is back. This time Frau Erika addresses him as "My dearest prince." After a very lyrical opening passage in which the stars in the heavens figure prominently, she eventually gets to the meaty part: "Thrills of joy (underlined in light blue) flooded the fairy soul's garment as news arrived, through the prince's letter, that the pact has now been sealed. The moment of bliss, when two pairs of lips met through the medium of roses, was brought back to the here and now by the energy of desire. Melting flutes resounded—violins rejoiced—an organ rumbled: the prelude to a symphony of peerless beauty! Did you feel it—the melody of our dreams? (New paragraph.) Write to me, my prince, about what you experienced as your lips touched that spot seemingly of paper, in truth, however, pulsing with life. (New paragraph.) The fairy tale is drawing nearer. The dusky handmaiden seems to place her trust in the fairy. Today she tried on clothing. A sweet little sweater, beige with red, was given to her as a present. The prince was also talked about. He impresses because he's natural and kind—and because he wants to get ahead in life. About men in general she says they are only desirous of a girl's body; a girl's soul, her words, they trod upon heedlessly. On top of it all, they balk at marriage! By this (underlined in light blue) she means the menial! Prince, be shrewder than he! This your Fairy Godmother counsels you."

Fireside Chat

Viktor's work is disrupted over the weekend by the ruthlessly noisy training course. The short-term guests, having no respect for the peace and quiet of New Glory, whistle their way through the halls, come pounding down the stairs, and shout jokes from window to window. The breaks in between, when they're allowed to get rowdy, are seemingly the highlight of the training course. Even when they gather in the dining room for instruction, their laughter can be heard all over the house. Olga and Thilde complain the most about them: they track dirt into the building, make lewd comments toward the women, and are constantly griping. The regular guests, for their part, have to put up with clogged toilets and flooded bathrooms, and it breaks Frau Erika's heart to see the potted plants being used as ashtrays. The only person in good spirits is Max. Not wanting to openly admit that he actually prefers the commotion and noise to the usual monotony, he points out to the complainers that they have a Plan to meet, which is only possible, he adds, when the place is full and sales are good—particularly drinks, which he procures unflaggingly. He sees to it that beer is available at breakfast on a self-serve basis, and since the participants readily avail themselves of it, things get so lively in the dining room in the morning that the regular guests couldn't possibly be expected to share the room with them. Thus, Frau Erika and Köpke take breakfast in their rooms, whereas Viktor is allowed, for the very first time, to take a seat at the kitchen table.

Unfortunately, he rarely gets a glimpse of Thilde, who's helping Olga serve. Since his offers to help have been declined (he's allowed to time the eggs, no more), he's forced to lend his ear to Max, who grumbles (while trying to shove cold cuts between Püppi's sealed lips) about the women, who always seem to forget what the training courses are like. The wailing starts when one is announced, it increases as soon as the guests arrive, but then when the guests go home it turns into mourning, because everyday life sets in again. Weekends like these are a joy and a nuisance in one. "You'll find out for yourself, Comrade Kösling."

And Max is right. Apart from Köpke, who stays under the radar and is probably roaming the woods all day, everyone gets caught up in the commotion, most of all Viktor, who proves himself this Saturday night—as the son of a VIP, as a speaker, a dancer, and a lover.

Viktor's impression of the course participants as nothing but barbarian intruders is soon abandoned once they recognize and begin to admire him. At first, all he notices is their curious, seemingly unintentional glances, until a stouthearted girl approaches him and asks if it's true what people are saying about him. Before long, he is surrounded by a throng of men and women and is able to demonstrate how, as the son of a big shot, one's fate can be borne with aplomb and dignity. He's spurred on by the fact that Thilde, who's busy clearing the tables, is keeping tabs on what's going on. Without being coy, he shows his modesty by indicating that he's embarrassed by all the attention he's getting. When he does share something about himself, he clearly endeavors to divert the conversation away from his person. He makes an effort to reciprocate the attention they show him; the questions they ask he asks in return. And he suggests to the people who find him interesting that it's no less interesting for him to learn about them.

The people he's dealing with, he eventually finds out, are hobby and amateur journalists—scribblers, in other words, who fill up the last page or two of the newspaper with articles about chess, stamp collecting, model trains, aquariums, antiques, spices, and puzzles. The young woman who was daring enough to open the conversation introduces herself as a specialist in flowers for home and garden, in common parlance a florist, and since Viktor is somewhat familiar with flowers, compared, say, to coins, he latches on to her comment and succeeds in winning the hearts of those around him. He not only comes up with the epithet "crucial dabs of color in our leafy-treed forests," but also the assertion that the low esteem this line of journalism is accorded is by no means commensurate to its real importance.

His comment strikes a chord. He's hit on the very thing that concerns them all and that invariably becomes the unofficial topic at every professional gathering, much to the chagrin of their course instructors. Their collective inferiority complex is promptly put on display for Viktor, keeping him busy for the next couple of hours—because he can't resist the florist's request to listen to her speech, and likewise has to stand by Matthi when he delivers his. Although the first—on the prickly topic of Floristics in the Press: Yes or No?—is answered with a resounding yes, and the second talk takes a look at domestic policy issues in light of the umpteenth plenum, the follow-up discussion deals almost exclusively with the general disregard for their work. The applause Viktor draws after using other words to repeat their lament from a layman's perspective spurns him on to propose a salutatory address to the highest administrative body in which the assembled participants' grievances, cleverly packaged as declarations of consent, are given official voice. He dashes off the appropriate words and phrases in the blink of an eye, so that all the course instructor has to do is jot them down. He dismisses their gratitude and applause with a modest wave of his hand. And yet he knows full well how good he was—and hopes that Thilde was witness to his triumph through the open kitchen door. He's the kind of person, he plans on telling her when he gets the chance, who needs other people to reach his full potential; books, by contrast, which isolate you from social contacts, can easily make you—or him, at least—unproductive.

He can't pursue his thoughts about the social impulses that inspire him because the impulses still happen to be working strong. The floral specialist, in particular, is all over him. She's compelled to tell him about the positive influence that houseplants can have on one's overall outlook on life. Even at supper she doesn't let up. He eventually manages to extricate himself in order to go change for the farewell party.

All employees and guests are invited to the celebration. It promises to be a good time, but it begins with cultural gravitas: Frau Erika Schulze-Decker will talk about the life of her husband. In the schedule of events, this item bears the subtitle "Fireside Chat." And sure enough, there's a fireplace for Frau Erika to sit down by—her own portable one, that is, requiring neither wood nor fire. Helgalein, who's been here since morning, set it up in the lounge, where normally at this hour Köpke would be sitting in front of the television. Her listeners huddle around the flickering electric flame. Even the window sills are occupied. That's where the florist is sitting, having planted herself within eyeshot of Viktor. This is something Viktor should, in all fairness, be able to understand, having chosen his own seat because of the view it affords him. Thus, while Viktor's profile is being studied, his own eyes are glued to another. The reciprocal gazes expected of him he hopes for no less avidly himself, albeit from another pair of eyes, dark-brown ones.

Max, looking solid in his suit and tie, escorts the leading lady into the room. He pulls up a chair to the fireplace for her, stands waiting till quiet sets in, and does not give a welcome address as Viktor feared but merely intimates a bow and withdraws. Silence fills the air for a few brief seconds before Frau Schulze-Decker begins her talk, calmly and quietly at first, then loud and shrill when emotion overwhelms her. Because even though, as she herself points out, she had no part in the feats of her husband, she is there in her heart, vicariously—and this she puts on public display, at times pathetic, at times sentimental. Her listeners, referred to as "my dear young friends," are hardly bored. They may have heard heroic tales of the Schulze-Decker type a thousand times before, but never performed so fervently: at once inspiring and comical. No one notices that the elderly bleach-blond lady doesn't keep her initial promise to present not a mythical hero but a human being in flesh and blood with all the attendant strengths and weaknesses.

The operetta-trilling lass in a dirndl and the letter-writing fay of roses don't even enter Viktor's head when he sees the elderly lady comrade elegantly dressed in black. The question which of these is the real Frau Erika is far from his mind right now. He has more important things to do, like observing a nose which boldly juts forward under thick eyebrows, ending in a gentle curve at the tip; he has to take note of lips which are pulled in periodically then unfurl their moistly shimmering splendor; he has to count how often the anticipated gazes just graze him and how often and how long they come to rest on him; he has to send (because it pains him to disappoint people) an occasional glance toward the window, too; above all, though, he has to devise a plan for the moment the talk is over, the fire goes out, and everyone streams into the dining room next door, where Max has provided a variety of drinks on a self-serve basis.

The applause following Frau Schulze-Decker's closing exhortation—to not only honor the dead but to prove oneself worthy through deeds—is friendly but brief. Everyone speedily crowds the exit. Shouting over the noise, the course instructor asks them to take their chairs with them. Viktor naturally follows orders, losing a degree of mobility in the process; with a chair in his arm he finds it difficult to snake his way through the crowd. He watches as the individual to whom he'd planned on posing the eminently important question, How's Tita doing? disappears chairlessly, while another, whom he wanted to avoid, reaches him with ease (furniture-free), gives him a hearty squeeze on the arm, and says, as if it were settled, "See you on the dance floor, right?"

Viktor is replying in the affirmative to the flower girl when he notices Helgalein waving in his direction. Together with chair, he extricates himself from the crowd and goes back to the fireplace, where Frau Erika, exhausted but content, is still sitting. "Well?" she asks, waiting for him to shower her with compliments, something Viktor is never at a loss for. While Helgalein turns off the fireplace, wraps up the extension cord, and carries them back upstairs, her sister keeps pressing Viktor for praise. But his alone is not enough. She wants to hear what the others have to say and plans to head to the dance floor to find out—in Viktor's accompaniment, it goes without saying. Before he can think of an excuse, Helgalein the organizer has already set up an appointment for him: he's to report to her room in half an hour, after her coffee and dress break.

DECEIVER DECEIVED

This is a rowdy chapter. Everything that happens in it the reader has to imagine as being blanketed by noise. Everything that's said is said loudly, and still not always comprehensible. Sebastian claims that under such conditions even mental and bodily movements require more effort than normal because you have to struggle against the background noise. It's thick like oatmeal porridge, he says, impeding forward motion; it blinds you like fog, makes breathing an ordeal, and causes the organism as a whole to suffer. Thinking, speaking, and listening become more difficult, making communication all but impossible. What's more, far from being a regrettable side effect, all of this is the unacknowledged aim. No small amount of money is spent to supply the equipment for acoustic torment. You submit to it voluntarily, gladly letting it numb your senses. Individuality is obliterated by the racket; in collective frenzy you wiggle under a rhythmic whip. Sebastian calls it masochistic reveling, an expression of self-hatred, the attempt to drown out the pain of a life misspent with a different kind of pain.

Viktor, who knows nothing of masochists and catches only bits and pieces of this discourse on noise (on account of the noise), understands Sebastian only partially but doesn't hesitate to gainsay him—not because he wants to express his opinion but because he wants to impress Thilde. Thilde's face clearly expresses her uneasiness about the gardener's grumbling: she's not about to let a good time on the dance floor be blackened by his gloominess. Viktor, then—whose viewpoint on the issue can be reduced to the formula: Where he lives, everything really existing is well and good!—manages despite the deafening noise to distance himself, in all honesty, from the prophet of doom by boldly asserting, "Let the people have some fun!"

This three-way conversation takes place outside the door to Thilde's room. Viktor, having stopped by to pose his question about Tita's well-being, finds Sebastian there already. Sebastian, for all his disparaging words, has come to pick up Thilde for the dance. But Thilde doesn't want to leave the apartment until Tita, who's plagued by bouts of anxiety, falls asleep. She could lock the doors, says Sebastian gruffly, but Tita—Thilde points out, annoyed—knows how to open the windows.

The atmosphere, in other words, is already tense when Viktor arrives. It only gets worse with Sebastian's anti-noise discourse, which in Thilde's eyes is a direct assault on her longing to dance. Sebastian clearly has the advantage in the tiff that ensues. As an opponent of noise, his only motivation for heading straight to its source is his desire to please Thilde, whereas she, a lover of noise, is purportedly tied down with Tita.

Viktor recognizes the opportunity immediately. He'll sacrifice personal pleasure this evening for the sake of long-term goals; by allowing his rival an apparent advantage for now, he'll assure himself of victory later. His starting position is good. After all, his reason for stopping by was his concern for Tita. Now that he hears about the state she's in, it's only natural for him to offer to look after her. He proposes the following. He'll disengage himself from Frau Erika, who's waiting for him as he speaks, as soon as possible so he can sit up with Tita, all night if need be. For him, it is no sacrifice at all. He's more than willing to do it for Tita. He's even looking forward to a game or two. And if that doesn't work out, he's got more than enough work to keep him busy.

He doesn't wait for Thilde to thank him. Seconds later he's standing at Frau Erika's door. The ladies are ready for action, both of them clad to their ankles in velvet. They've been having champagne, not a coffee break; this explains their giddiness. A glass is filled for Viktor, then the bottle is empty. He escorts the two ladies down the stairs and across the yard, Helgalein with her shot-putter's figure in navy blue on his left, the petite Frau Erika draped in youthful yellow on his right. Having praised their velvet outfits, he receives a lecture (noise level permitting) about clothing, which not only lends expression to the inner disposition of its wearer but has a determining influence on it as well. He already knows that the soul is material and the material is soul, so it hardly surprises him to hear that, for one thing, the colors or lack of colors you wear on the outside rub off on your insides and, for another, that worries, joys, and thoughts penetrate your clothing and are stored inside them so there's an ever-present danger that putting on old clothes will infect the wearer with old worries, cares, and worn-out thoughts, in short, mental detritus. Thus, rule numero uno: wear only new clothing. If for some reason this isn't possible, then each occasion should at least have its own special garment. A dress uniform does not belong on the battlefield just as overalls have no place at a party; black, which may be appropriate for a lecture on the deceased, can spread the smell of decay at a ball. With every day being full of events, your wardrobe has to be full of clothing. Thus, rule number two: change your clothing as often as possible every day. Getting old has a lot to do with the clothing you wear. If you only ever wear dark colors, you're essentially courting death—one foot in the grave, so to say. The resulting rule number three is spoken by Frau Erika but no one hears it, because they're drawing near to the dining-room door.

No sooner do they enter the haze of cigarette smoke and beer fumes than Viktor's companions begin to wriggle rhythmically under the influence of the music. Clapping their hands and howling for joy, they hurl themselves into the crowd, where Max, somewhat in his cups already but nonetheless still steady on his feet, takes them under his wing. Viktor, who's cut himself loose under the pretext of finding a place for them to sit, pilots himself back toward the door but doesn't get far, because someone with a firm grip takes hold of his arm.

The florist has followed rule number two as well, exchanging pants and leather jacket for skirt and blouse. She gets as close to Viktor as humanly possible, says something to him, then repeats it when he doesn't understand her because of the noise. When all he does

93

is shrug his shoulders, she puts her mouth to his ear and, instead of speaking, kisses it. Viktor thanks her with a smile but indicates that, unfortunately, he has to leave her for a moment. He frees himself from her grip, gives her a look that is meant to be promising, and disappears. Only when he reaches the yard does he wipe the moisture off his ear.

Thilde is busy putting Tita to bed, so Viktor finds only Sebastian in her room. The gardener immediately grabs the books Viktor brought with him, flips through them, and starts to gripe again. He doesn't like the word *work*, which Viktor used to describe his reading. For him, the term has something to do with sense, purpose, and usefulness, but what Viktor has in mind here is the epitome of sense-less-ness. The fifty or even a hundred books Viktor has dragged along with him he'll merely use to create a new one, which will only serve, in turn, to provide material for future doctoral candidates. If technological progress only serves to free up productive labor for running on the spot—and we have every reason to fear that it does—then it's not worth more than the whole of our cud-chewing educational system, whose pervasiveness, by the way, the budding doctor would do well to think about once in a while.

Sentiments of this sort are hardly as foreign to Viktor as Sebastian assumes. Although he never actually thought them himself, he *could* have thought them, because it's obvious that he's often looking for a way to explain his reluctance to work. He therefore resolves to turn Sebastian's thoughts into arguments of his own. He'd still like to find out what the gardener's thoughts are on history in particular but doesn't get around to asking because he now has to admire a Sunday dress. He does so (well aware that the best compliments aren't witty but spontaneous) by crying out, "How beautiful you are!"—which is honest enough, but only refers to the person and not the flowered outfit, which disfigures rather than dignifies its wearer.

Viktor still has to greet Tita, Thilde having told her that Viktor would be taking care of her this evening. He's startled by her face, corpselike without its teeth. She lies there prim and proper in a wool nightgown, arms resting on the covers, cordially returns his greeting, and says, "Very kind of you!" when he offers her a few cheerful words.

She only becomes irritable when he tells her who he is: "I may be a little funny in the head but I'm not so dumb that I don't know you're the doctor." She rubs her eyes like a child to indicate her urge to sleep, and Viktor tiptoes out of the room. Once she's asleep, Thilde explains, the danger is over and he can leave his post. But this he wouldn't think of. Even if Tita doesn't make a scene in the middle of the night—although he's hoping she does, for the opportunity to prove his worthiness—he plans to stay put until Thilde gets back. He won't be bored with all of his books. Here in her room, knowing that he's sure to see Thilde again without even having to make an effort, he can work with the utmost calm and concentration.

Without the slightest hesitation, he begins to peruse the random selection of books he brought with him: volumes containing letters written by the Prussian king from the years pertaining to Viktor's research. Having listened one last time at Tita's door, he opens the first volume, intent on reading it systematically. Skipping the foreword, which is of little interest to him, he reads the heading of section one: "Letters from the King to His Ambassadors in Paris"—and thereby reaches the end of his tether. Because, apart from the words *monsieur*, *madame*, and *bonjour*, the language used by the King of Prussia to communicate with his officials is entirely foreign to Viktor. He looks for translations in the mass of footnotes and in the appendix, discovers there are none, but doesn't despair. Having just gotten into his stride, he takes a sheet of paper, and pens the word "Preliminaries!" across the top of it, jotting down item number one: Have Mother find a translator! Not a sound can be heard from Tita's room, so he heads to his room to fetch some other reading material, books he's capable of understanding.

He doesn't get very far, however. Helgalein blocks his way at the landing, cheeks aflush from drinking and dancing. "Where have you been!" she rebukes with a smile. Helgalein can't help it, all the time grinning in spite of herself. She's just as gleeful as everyone else, Manuela and Olga included. Everyone, the whole kit and caboodle, is there. Only Viktor and Thilde are missing. The drinking contest is over, the eating contest is about to begin, then it's time for the conga line, and our scholar certainly doesn't want to miss out on that.

The formidable little sister, who talks Berlinese as soon as Frau Erika isn't around, is relentless in her appeals to dance. Ever smiling, and raving about the variety of amusements to be had, she accompanies Viktor up to his room, allows him only to unload his useless reading matter, then drags him to the place of merriment, which heat, smoke, and noise have transformed into a veritable hell.

The tables have all been pulled together and almost everyone familiar by now to Viktor and the reader is gathered around. Only Thilde is missing. That Sebastian is absent too is noticed only by Viktor, a realization followed by a severe and diffuse pain previously unknown to him which he attempts to assuage by disputing its legitimacy. Nothing, absolutely nothing, he tells himself, has come to pass between Thilde and him as yet. There's no reason for the suffering he feels (where exactly: in his head? in his chest?), and yet it increases as he comes to understand that the garret has never been as safe as it is right now, what with the loud and penetrating music absorbing every other sound around. "Thilde," he announces over the din of the music, surprised at the assuredness in his voice, "is unable to come. As much as it pains her, she can't leave Tita."

At first, he thinks the pain will go away as quickly as it came. When the opposite occurs, however, and the agony only intensifies, he begins to battle against it. He soon puts an end to the disagreeable condition of being the only sober one in the room. He dances up a storm, constantly switching partners and assuring each and every one of them that it's only worth dancing with her. With no resistance from Max, who's called the tune until now, he nominates himself conga-line organizer and comes up with the craziest ideas. He lines people up in an orderly fashion, according to shoe size, height, and bust, has them roll up their pant legs and put pots on their heads, and makes them jump over hurdles while dancing. Then the human snake, led by Viktor, marches festively through cold and snow, into the warmth of the cowshed, followed (as if to heighten his never-ending torment) by the main building, through the door and up the stairs—but only to the first floor, where Frau Erika stands a round of champagne before saying her adieus: "Go on without me, kiddies. I'm beat."

When Viktor, back downstairs in hell, tries to quench his infernal anguish through systematic swilling, he comes to learn that feelings are more resistant than thoughts and the power of recollection. At some point, without knowing how he got there, he finds himself back in his room, but not alone.

Neither pain nor florist have been banished by alcohol. He accepts her solicitations obligingly. Too late does he notice that it only intensifies his suffering rather than alleviating it, and Flora, as he calls her (her real name, in fact, is Margarete), never notices at all. She, the ensnarer, is all too reminiscent of all the other women for whom he's often felt what his paucity of words called *love*. Yes, surely, he thinks, while sinking into her as if into something familiar and intimate, this, too, is called love, even though it has nothing to do with the new, the powerful, the unfamiliar sensation which mercilessly torments him even now. However unjust, he can't help but compare: that which is happening now with that which is yet to come. The pairs of opposites—small-big, shallow-deep, ordinary-sensational—are too weak to capture his feelings. He searches for images, scours the globe, no, the entire universe, to get an idea of what the momentous finale will be once his intensive agony is transformed into intensive pleasure.

Not for a minute does he forget that it's Flora whose reality is nourishing his visions. But the emotional deception he's perpetrating against her doesn't burden his conscience, because she doesn't suspect a thing. Her trust in him is remarkable. He finds this moving—an emotion he deftly combines with thankfulness into a declaration that sounds like happiness and that stimulates her own, the genuine kind. This spurs him on, in turn, to put on a display of rapture and delight that is so realistic he almost believes it himself. He'd like to create in Flora at least an inkling of the happiness that's awaiting him elsewhere in the future. It's not only his sense of justice that compels him to do so; at work here is also the insatiable desire to be loved, which even the agony of having to love someone back hasn't managed to smother.

Success makes clear to him just how hopelessly he's succumbed to his agony. When Flora clings to him, half crying, half laughing, calls him her one and only, her darling and dearest, whom she knew at first glance was Mr. Right, swears to him that never in her life has she been so happy, not even in her wildest dreams, explains to him in the plainest terms that she'll get a divorce the moment he calls her name, begs him to tell her right now, for God's sake, when, where, and how she'll be able to relive this newfound glory as soon as possible—at the mention of all these things, the pleasure Viktor normally expects suddenly fails to materialize. All that's there is a wistful memory: of a time when nothing was left to be desired, when he could warm himself at the fire he'd kindled.

Joyful Emergency

Alas, strong incentives to get to work come to Viktor at a time when they're unable to bear fruit. They emanate from Thilde, yet reach Viktor in a roundabout way through Sebastian, who, neatly splitting a tire-sized block of pine with one fell swoop of an axe, comments on Thilde in a tone of regret: sadly, she's not content with her present state of being; she's always thinking about her future.

Little does Sebastian suspect how much this sentence will preoccupy Viktor and affect his future behavior. For Sebastian, Thilde is not the point; he's just using her as a model. The issue at hand is no less than happiness itself. And since Thilde, if you're to believe his interpretation, embodies the opposite of happiness, he can use her (while chopping wood) as proof of the fact that the desire for change is guaranteed to lead straight to the depths of dissatisfaction.

It's hard for Viktor to say how long he's been at New Glory when he gains this insight into Thilde's inner world; he's completely lost track of the days. He knows neither what day of the week it is nor which day of the month. Time has slipped through his fingers unaccounted for since the forces of nature have taken over. Icy storms have brought masses of snow from the polar regions, traffic is jammed from southern Sweden clear to the Central German Uplands, power lines are down, snowed-in villages are being supplied by helicopters, and yet Vikor leads the carefree existence of a child of nature, living for the day, however short. His thoughts scarcely veer beyond this tiny fleck in the snowy expanse of Europe called New Glory (which no one supplies, by airlift or otherwise). He's glad the phones are dead and isn't bothered that the mail goes undelivered, since he isn't expecting any. When the power goes out on top of it all, it seems to him like a dream come true.

The other denizens of New Glory aren't exactly panicky either when the only news from the outside world reaches them via Viktor's battery-operated transistor radio. Fear, if there is any, is not on display. They trust in the imminent triumph of standard climatic conditions in the temperate zone in which they reside and are told by Olga, two times, three times, over and over, that her food supplies are crisis-proof. It's also a relief knowing that the neighboring villages can be reached on foot if need be. Sebastian undertook the strenuous trek already, in Viktor's company, when the power went out. They went to buy candles, which, of course, were not available. Luckily, Frau Erika has plenty of ornamental candles she's been saving up for festive occasions, and sparingly hands out with a reminder about the positive sides of sitting in the dark. A waxen rose casts a meager glow in Viktor's room but is seldom put to use—not because Viktor follows Frau Erika's advice, using his room to let his inner light shine in the darkness, but because he only uses his room to sleep in. Apart from that he spends his time elsewhere. For an emergency not only makes people equal and frugal; it makes them sociable, too.

It was thanks to Köpke that the impending calamity didn't catch the rest home napping on Sunday, the day after the raucous party. Köpke slept through the night with the help of sedatives, went on a lengthy march through the woods at the crack of dawn, and then, with staff and guests still sound asleep, tried to forget his morning hunger by parking himself in front of the TV. When he heard the news that Jutland and Holstein were snowed under, Rügen and Rostock no longer accessible, he saw his chance to finally get some breakfast and alerted the staff and guests. So seriously did they take his warning that all of the short-term guests (Helgalein included) up and left New Glory before lunch. With the exception of Max, who'd bought mounds of cake for their afternoon coffee, no one was sad to see them go—least of all Viktor. He didn't wave as Flora departed, didn't show up for lunch or dinner. Appearing in the yard with snow shovel in hand on Monday morning, he'd slept (interrupted by the occasional semiconscious stupor) for nearly twenty hours.

Viktor is one of those people who can sleep just about anywhere—except next to someone else. A floor, bench, or chair will give him a better night's rest than a bed in which he is not the sole occupant. The euphemism "to sleep with so and so" is one he never uses; it's too far removed from reality for him, if not a mendacious notion. By his own lights, love and sleep have nothing to do with each other, are in fact mutually exclusive, like love and sickness or love and death, which also occur in the same place but which no one mixes metaphorically like he does when a peaceful sleeper is lying next to him and he, the one in need of sleep, feels utterly sick from sleeplessness. Experience has taught him that his own views, born of his inability to sleep, are not shared by females. Suggestions to sleep in separate beds during the passive hours of the night have always been construed as a sign of his coldheartedness. So he suffers in silence, though not without the feeling of being victimized by fate; for if pain is the price of pleasure, there's no reason why he should have to bear the brunt of it.

And that's exactly how it played out the night of the party. Sleeping skin to skin was deemed a sign of love, whereas the cautious mention of Flora's empty bed in the room behind the stairs was nothing short of sacrilege. Viktor's assertion that love can only be felt in a waking state was rebutted with a reference to a physical instinct independent of consciousness. And it soon became clear that this wasn't the mystical nonsense Viktor assumed it to be. Because whenever he was on the point of carrying out a detailed plan of escape to the pair of chairs next to the stove, his every move thought out in advance, the breathing pattern of the slumbering woman at his side would suddenly be disrupted, she'd mumble a term of endearment for him, and an arm or leg would wrap itself around him, effectively pinning him down. The reflex (which Viktor christened the unconscious drive for possession) worked so flawlessly that by the time the late-morning snow alert came, Flora had slept about six, her lover not a single hour.

No one, then, was more grateful to the watchful Köpke than Viktor. He lovingly made the bed he regained after a hasty farewell, started and ended the day with a visit to the bathroom, then went into hibernation—to awake on Monday a different man. The rest-home guest has now become its hostage; the doctoral candidate has suddenly morphed into an emergency worker. Career and dissertation, father and mother—none of this matters anymore. Light, heat, and food are of the essence now. Instead of the calendar, he consults the thermometer; instead of studying history, he learns how to saw and split wood. And when he calls it work, Sebastian is no longer offended.

Work is never lacking. The snow makes sure of that, falling without cease, being heaped up in the yard into walls higher than the shovelers before eventually having to be carted out in front of the gate. Later the automatic watering machine in the cowshed freezes up, so that water has to be carried from the kitchen across the farm-yard. With coal supplies getting low, the logs stacked up behind the cowshed have to be turned into firewood. From his vast collection of engines, Max has converted an old diesel to power the cordwood saw. The children drag up the logs, Viktor takes them off their hands and passes them on to Sebastian, who feeds them carefully into the blade, its steel teeth screeching through them. The wind, still blowing, whirls up sawdust; mixed with snow, it sticks to eyes and noses. Although hands and feet are always in motion, no one manages to keep them warm. Only when darkness sets in and the saw goes silent can they carry on their conversations again; until then they communicate with sign language. Back inside, in the toasty kitchen, everyone talks in their loudest voice, their ears still deaf from the noise of the saw. They sit around a candle, eat their fill, drink their coffee, then eat some more. They smoke, chat, drink schnapps, and pass on infectious yawns. Max argues with Olga, Sebastian lectures, Püppi screams, and Tita, who's fit and well again, starts to croon old songs. When she gets to her favorite, the one about the changeable moon, Thilde and Manuela sing along while Viktor assumes the role of poet, filling in the missing lines with invented ones of his own.

Max and Olga are not alone in their griping. Viktor joins them, in the foulest language he's capable of, complaining about the weather and the grueling work; he does so in silence, for himself alone, but it makes him feel good all the same. If it were up to him, he often thinks, the calamity needn't end soon. The snow has not only buried the roads, fields, and woods, but his bad conscience as well. He can now focus his energies wholly on what he calls the essentials. From morning till evening he devises plans in his mind, revises, discards, or evaluates them. His mind is active like never before; he's living in a constant state of anticipation and is not disappointed either, since he knows how to downsize his expectations. Indeed, things are not moving along very briskly for him and his dark-haired objective. But the pace is sufficient. Perhaps it's a result of the unchanging weather, but he has the feeling of having an infinite amount of time on his hands, doesn't rush things, and is satisfied with baby steps. Sometimes he even thinks he can do without those, that the present state of affairs is wholly sufficient. Three times a day, at mealtimes, he can count on seeing Thilde. What's more, his concern for Tita is reason enough for an occasional discussion. He's taken on the task of carrying kindling and coal to the rooms, and when other chores aren't pressing, he relieves the stove-stoker of her ash-removal duties as well. Having a chat at one stove or another has turned into a pleasant routine for him. The topics vary but the general tendency is toward the more personal—though only from his side for now, not hers. He's careful to hold back the many questions he'd like to ask her, for he doesn't want to importune. She, for her part, is full of curiosity. She'd like to know how they live where Kösling's son comes from. Her questions seem to stem from a sociological interest. He formulates his answers accordingly but always uses one and the same example to illustrate them: himself. In tiny, sometimes humorous, sometimes somber episodes, he offers her random bits and pieces of his life. If she wants, she can piece them together. More important, however, she can learn from him how to let her hair down. He doesn't openly encourage her to do so; he merely sets an example. He tries to win her confidence by offering up his own.

Since everyone at the table drank the pledge of friendship at Olga's behest, he now calls Thilde by her first name. They avoided the customary kiss, as though in secret agreement. They didn't even talk about it, nor did they talk about another minor matter which (so he

103

hopes) conjoins them. Thilde had disclosed to him her suspicion that men with facial hair are extremely vain, whereupon Viktor parted from his the very next morning. If she understood and accepted his tribute, she certainly didn't let on to it. Whatever the case, she didn't share in the hilarity caused by his clean-shaven face.

Viktor's object lesson in trust has not had the desired effects, so of course he's grateful for any information about Thilde he can glean from other sources. Tita is not very useful in this respect, since she only repeats what he knows already. Olga and Max have nothing but preformed opinions to offer. Both of them, each in their own way, are caught up in the notion that Thilde thinks she's superior: for Max she's a know-it-all, for Olga she's hoity-toity, disguising her pride behind a veneer of quiet friendliness. He never talks about Thilde with Frau Erika, but they do still write, however sporadic and sluggish their correspondence may be. Frau Erika hasn't gotten anywhere with the chambermaid, neither in terms of exploring her soul nor as a suitor's accomplice. The core of this soul, she writes, is locked away like no other. The fairy godmother is at a loss but hopes that a man like the prince will end up having the key that fits. Köpke never talks about people at all, only about deer and TV shows, so the only other potential source of information is, of all people, Sebastian. And while it's true that his mouth is always running, he invariably picks the topics himself. Hence Viktor is condemned to wait.

For days he chops wood with Sebastian, listens to monologues about the sad state of the earth, which technological madness is disfiguring today and destroying tomorrow, wields whetstone, file, wedge, axe, and hatchet, learns how to position the block of wood (called a bolt) and where it has to be hit to split easily, collects the pieces in baskets and stacks them, can soon distinguish the heavy, hard woods like oak and acacia from the soft, light ones like birch and poplar, tries with eyes closed to recognize the different types of wood by their smell, looks on in wonderment at how the yellowish alder turns reddish after splitting—and suddenly gives a start as Sebastian, in the midst of a lengthy speech about the true (that is, the simple) pleasures in life, finally utters the long-awaited name: people like *Thilde*, he says with a swing of the axe, who set more store by the future than the present, are setting themselves up to be miserable, because living for the future means not living at all; the future is nonexistent, reality only exists in the present.

Now, the reader would be wrong to assume that an easily influenced Viktor willingly submits to Sebastian's every view. In fact, the opposite is true. Contrariness stirs inside him, for it's not Sebastian's overt opinions that are crucial to him but the ideas Sebastian conveys without even realizing or intending it. When Viktor learns that Thilde is not content with what she is and has but is obsessed with the idea of change and wants to move on, move up, or get ahead, the very same drive takes hold of *him*, and he begins collecting the words he'll need to express it in the most original terms

By skillfully wielding the insights filtered out of Sebastian's polemics, the stove-side chat that takes place the following morning turns out to be a success. For the very first time, Thilde takes a crack at countering Viktor's personal statements with declarations of her own, which, admittedly, don't pan out so well. The attempt is prompted by Viktor's painfully subdued lamentations: his mental inactivity, which he claims is forced, is slowly becoming unbearable for him; the sluggish progress on his dissertation is tearing holes in his plans and driving him insane; the sight of unread books in his room fills him with despair, and it's hard for him not to let it show. "Can you tell?" To which Thilde responds, "No, but you can't tell with me either," indicating that she expects him to ask her candidly about her own variety of despair. And when the questions come, she answers them—or tries to, at least, first by broadly describing Viktor's situation as rosy compared with hers, then by becoming more specific but less to the point, until Viktor helps her along with questions. He puts on a face to match the bitterness of her words, inwardly exults in his success at having gotten her to open up, and is ultimately disturbed by what she says. For Thilde talks about baking and travel.

Both, of course, are examples of what is lacking in her life, symbols for something that's hard for her to describe. Indeed, her problems with language are not only limited to the letter *s* and grammar (whose rules she sometimes breaks, mixing up cases the way Tita does) but also include her choice of words, particularly when it comes to describing her inner life. Complaining is something she hasn't practiced. Before Viktor came, she later tells him, there was never a need for her to talk about herself because there was no one to take an interest in her unfathomable inner workings. Hence, she's unable to talk about her feelings, or at least has a hard time doing so; she can't find the words to express what she means. She gropes for things she faintly intuits, starts with details, collects and sorts them—in the hope that, when all is said and done and the pieces of the puzzle have come together, something like an outline will emerge, along with the idea she's looking for.

Thus, her attempt to respond to Viktor begins with her love of baking. She talks about crescent rolls and crispy buns, streusel cake and meringue Chantilly—to Viktor's considerable wonderment. (He had expected grander visions, like cancer therapy or rabies prevention.) She's more concerned with the baking process than with eating the results. She wants to be able to say: I made those myself! when everyone's mouth is watering. Even as a child, baking was her constant desire, but only as a child was she allowed to do it. Baking was strictly forbidden in the nurses' dormitory, and when she went back home, she had to contend with Olga, who doesn't let anyone near her kitchen utensils, as Viktor well knows.

Eager to capitalize on the lull that ensues, Viktor claims to have a hankering for plum cake—which doesn't make much of an impression on Thilde. "I was just saying," she replies, meaning baking was just one example. She starts in with another example: travel. She's been prohibited from doing so for a long time now and will be for a long time to come; Viktor knows why. And as she's busy describing—in far too much detail—all the places around the world she's bent on seeing, he no longer thinks that the despair caused by the lack of an oven is hopelessly comical. Rather, he puts himself in her position, he understands and sympathizes with her, suggesting a name for the thing she's lacking: independence or perhaps freedom. She accepts his suggestion with an awkward smile, but remains skeptical, adding, "I'm not so sure," before bringing their conversation to a close with a figure of speech her grandmother uses: "No use complaining!"

Viktor notices for the first time that Thilde has the habit of placing her hand on her forehead when she's thinking. He's emboldened by the fact that the gesture reveals what her bangs are meant to hide: an inch-long red scar. Although it's not her intention to show him what she considers a flaw, he takes it as a sign of trust that it no longer occurs to her to hide it in his presence.

New Misery

The end of the snow emergency at New Glory marks the end of a period which, compared with what's to come, could be described as golden. In retrospect, the threat posed by nature proves to have had a protective function. People like Frau Erika who are inclined to attribute things to supernatural causes would recognize a higher purpose in the cold wave and snow: delaying the process of dissolution that immediately sets in once the roads to the outside world are opened. Griepenkerl, the blockade runner, witnesses a vivid demonstration of the process without comprehending it. Arriving from Görtz on a clear winter morning with tractor and snowplow, he was greeted at New Glory by the cheers of eight adults and four children. But when he calls on them again on the way back from Prötz in the hope of basking in his triumph one more time, he encounters only Olga, a screaming Püppi, and an agitated Frau Erika, who showers him with reproaches: his horsepower has cleared the way not only for new supplies but also for misfortune.

What Frau Erika refers to as misfortune has been commented on by others before her, with different words but in a similar vein. Thilde and Olga cried, Thilde in silence, Olga in sobs; Köpke, whose vacation is over, muttered something upon his departure about static interference; Sebastian came up with the name New Misery; and Max used words which for his sake won't be repeated here so as not to tarnish his memory. After all, he's taking his leave: from his workplace as well as this story.

The only one who doesn't share in the collective depression is Viktor. Although outwardly conforming to the emotional nadir, inwardly he's on top of the world. His heart's eye is focused on the heart of another. Everything outside of this purview is invisible, and everything he comes into contact with is judged according to its capacity to further or hinder the affairs of his heart. He's incapable of feeling for others because his emotional reserves are fully engaged. And since disaster for him has only one meaning, the morning's events are anything but disastrous; they're a chance for him to rise to the occasion.

No sooner has Griepenkerl's noisy vehicle set out from New Glory down the road to May Valley than the police arrive (much more stealthily) from Görtz. Two officers demand to see Max at once and have him show them around the garages. Police orders to remain in the house are obeyed by everyone except Püppi. By screaming her head off, she gains the right to join the tour of the garages on Papa's arm and is well behaved every step of the way. Only when they try to separate her from Max, who's been told to get in the car, does she lose control. Püppi clearly has no respect for state authorities. The man who gently pries her from Max's arms gets his face scratched. Viktor, who rushes to aid the bleeding man, has trouble holding the squirming child in his arm but is spared the wrath of her fingernails. Olga is told that she will learn the fate of her husband in no less than forty-eight hours. While the unscathed police officer inspects the wounds of his colleague, Max rolls down the window and shouts ill-natured remarks at a sobbing Olga. "You bitch!" he yells and declares that she hasn't seen the last of him. The policemen don't give him time to elaborate on his threat, however. He gets in only a few choice words appropriate to his predicament before the car, with him inside, rolls off into the winter landscape. Püppi cries out after him to the point of exhaustion, then falls asleep in Viktor's arms.

On top of this shock comes another shortly afterward: Thilde discovers that Tita has run away again. A meeting is convened in the kitchen to discuss a plan of action. That it takes so long is mostly Sebastian's fault. Despite having a driver's license and experience in dealing with the authorities, he refuses on principle to act as Max's

109

stand-in—giving Thilde reason to cry and Viktor the opportunity to display his magnanimity. Viktor not only offers to drive the car while Max is gone but sets himself up as the organizer of the search party. Whereas the others are more annoyed than concerned about Tita, cautioning against a large-scale search operation, advocating a wait-and-see strategy, and not even telling too-clever-by-half Thomas to watch his mouth when he parrots Max, saying it's time to stick the old lady in a home—Viktor, for his part, is indefatigably active. Since he knows what he wants (he wants to distinguish himself), he can pose as a leader and boost his authority. Reluctantly they obey as he assigns them their tasks. A submissive Gabi, quick to kiss up to him, is sent to search the house and yard. Thomas searches the surrounding area for clues, while Sebastian inquires after the runaway in Prötz and Arndtsdorf. Frau Erika is entrusted to keep watch on the telephone (still dead); the kitchen, the cows, and Püppi are tended to by Olga and Manuela, while the commander himself gets into Max's automobile and drives Thilde to Görtz before continuing on his own to the police.

Viktor is careful to conceal the exultant mood he's worked himself into, along with the fact that it's not his concern for Tita that's motivating him to act. Dropping Thilde off in Görtz and later picking her up there to help her inquire about Tita in Liepros, Schwedenow, and other villages, he never lets on that he's happy to be alone with her. He doesn't even utter the sentence that repeatedly crosses his mind: "I'm so glad I can help you!" He's not in for a quick fix; lasting success is what he's after, which is why he holds back his emotions and sticks to the program, the search for Grandma.

He's quick to note that Thilde is not the kind of person made talkative by worry. Even in fear she keeps quiet. It's up to Viktor to do the talking. And yet he's careful to restrain himself, since a too considerable command of words might only compound her inhibitions, or so he reasons. He wants his concern for Tita to be visible. This goes well with an awkwardly groping, occasionally disjointed manner of speech. Thus, he doesn't succumb to the temptation to soliloquize like Sebastian and is able to react to her mood so nimbly that his remarks often turn out to be an endorsement of what Thilde feels or thinks but doesn't say. In this way, he acts as a sounding board for her fears and is able to share her concerns.

And yet he can still pursue ulterior aims. It's no real challenge to direct the conversation to the topic of nursing homes. He never actually poses the question whether Tita should be institutionalized, but he does get Thilde to think about it—this or that, yes or no. Either way Viktor agrees. It goes without saying that he's careful to vary his affirmative stance; because uniformity, even if it expresses approval, runs the risk of resembling indifference. "Inconceivable!" he says from the depths of his heart as Thilde broaches the subject of nursing homes with the assertion that sending Tita to one would be a crime. "I don't doubt that, but still . . . !" he adds in a pensive, cautious tone as Thilde reflects on the unfortunate situation she finds herself in because of Tita. Then comes a self-critical declaration: "Quite right, I never thought about it that way," as the positive sides of a nursing home are enumerated. Finally, when what at first was called a crime has now been deemed a necessity, his silence (meant to convey distress) and a sigh are followed by his asking if there's really no alternative.

Viktor likewise has to suppress his impressions of nature, which he suddenly finds surprisingly moving. A snow-covered path through the woods or a lone tree standing in the field stir his emotions in a way not even the Crimea was able to. He would love to share them with Thilde, since his heightened emotional awareness and sensitivity are thanks to her, but he's afraid of offending her feelings, which are wholly fixated on her momentary fears and concerns. He therefore does so indirectly. He asks if Tita, when smitten with wanderlust, is still able to see, perhaps even admire her surroundings. He knows she can appreciate them otherwise, when she's clearheaded. He can remember well her delight in explaining to him the view from the family vault. Of course, she's on her own and can only enjoy it half as much, if at all, because to enjoy things wholly, he's recently discovered, it's important to share them with someone else. If he were driving, say, for example, past the peat lake right now without a companion and saw the glittering snowy surface of the lake behind the ruled lines of dried reeds and the blue sky above it, he would have to at least imagine telling someone about it, Thilde, for instance, if he wanted to enjoy the view at all.

His implicit (and obvious) question—whether Thilde feels the same—goes unanswered. Instead she yells "Stop!" She rushes to get out of the car and starts walking back the way they just came. She saw footsteps heading off the snow-plowed road and up a tree-lined hill. Viktor, having little desire to hike through the winter woods in his loafers, expresses his reservations about sleuthing around but is powerless against Thilde's hopefulness. Behind the hill, on Hoppschugge Dike, lives Frau Bahr, a distant relative whom Tita sometimes visits to have her cards read, which, of course, is nonsense. Viktor, who doesn't know the least thing about having your cards read, would like to find out more, but there's not enough time, for their cold-footed march is brief. Soon they pass under chestnut trees, through an overgrown garden where before them stands a tumbledown house, beset by bushes and flanked by walls of snow.

Frau Bahr, small and plump, sits in her fetid kitchen. The tomcat on her lap can't be bothered to get up, but the Pomeranian under the table vents its fury, snarling and barking its head off while Frau Bahr repeats: "Don't give up hope!" The woman who made the footsteps they followed is here too. She came from Schwedenow to bring food. Happy not having to return alone, she gladly tags along with them. Viktor drops her off at her doorstep.

The extent of Thilde's disappointment becomes apparent only when she's alone with Viktor again. He now witnesses for the very first time what it's like when she starts to cry: her tawny brown eyes fill up with water as her lips begin to tremble; she gulps down a sob, then another, and tries to take a deep breath before bursting soundlessly into a flood of tears.

She later apologizes to Viktor. He tells her he nearly cried along with her—which isn't remotely true. For his attempt to sympathize came to naught. Too great was his triumph at having her cry, unrestrained, in his presence.

Exchange of Glances

Viktor's feeling of triumph from the day's events intensifies during the night. At one or two in the morning he starts singing. The song about the changeable moon has particularly taken his fancy. It's a fitting tune, what with the full moon and the frosty night. He varies the tempo and melody as well as the lyrics: in his version, everything under the changeable moon should stay just the way it is.

He's alone in the car, and since the car is alone on the autobahn, he can run it as fast as it'll go. The noise level is therefore considerable, and Viktor has to sing loud to be heard. Only when he arrives at his destination and has to speak does he notice that his vocal cords have taken a beating. The uniformed guard wants to know what he's doing at a closed border crossing at this ungodly hour. Viktor answers in a croaking voice but is able to make himself understood. There's no need for him to explain in detail, since the reason for his coming is the same reason for the trouble they are experiencing here on the banks of the Oder. The man takes him to his superior, who, without wasting time on a welcome, puts on his cap and reads something official-sounding to Viktor in which an old woman's attempt to cross into Poland without her identity papers is referred to as a "border-crossing incident," and since the lady threatened the guard with a walking stick during their squabble, they add the word "armed." Her condition is described as nervous and unpredictable before the statement ends with the mention of a snack, proffered but left untouched.

Viktor's attempt to introduce a note of civility by offering praise, thanks, and explanations falls flat. Even his name, which he pronounces loud and clear, fails to elicit a response. Instead they ask to see his papers. He flashes his Foreign Ministry ID card in the hope of seeing their faces brighten, but no one here is interested in it; they want to see his personal identity card.

Although the barracks room they escort him to is overheated, Tita still has her coat and head scarf on. She sits erectly, cane between her knees. Recognizing Viktor at once, she says, "It's about time you came!" and scrambles to her feet. With the formal smile she reserves for strangers, she takes her leave of the men in uniform. Outside she sucks the cold air through her nostrils appreciatively, admires the moon—"Just like at the seaside, don't you think?"—then surprises Viktor with a hug, adding, "Ach, it's *so* good to have you back again!"

Ever since a sleep-deprived Frau Erika heard the restored telephone ringing and woke Viktor up in the middle of the night, he's been thinking about how to organize the big event: the reunion of Tita with her granddaughter. From radiant rescuer shouting for joy at Thilde's bedside with a smiling Tita on his arm to the humble helper who makes himself invisible after a deed accomplished because her thanks would put him to shame—he goes through all the roles and scenarios without being able to settle on one. He dreams himself into each and every one of them, savoring each in advance, but still hasn't come up with a reasonable plan. Tita, who doesn't speak during the ride back but doesn't sleep either, only bothers him once. "Say," she asks, "can you tell me who those men in green suits were and how I got there in the first place?"

The words Viktor eventually comes up with to offer a sleeping Thilde won't be spoken this evening because he never makes it to her bed. No sooner does he pull the car up into the yard than Frau Erika and Thilde come rushing outside, open the car door, and usher Tita into the house. Viktor, who also got out of the vehicle, is about to get in again and drive it into the garage when Thilde comes back out. They stand a good two yards apart from each other in moonlight and glittering snow. With words of thanks and words of welcome they furnish proof (Sebastian would say) of their being "domesticated," letting their eyes say what really matters.

Their dialogue of glances has given Viktor a brand-new experience: that motions of the soul can deprive you of your sleep. Whether his own eyes are open or shut, the other pair is always there. He doesn't think about her gaze, doesn't ruminate over how it came to be and what it means, he simply holds it (or it holds him), reproduces it over and over in his mind and, although he longs to sleep, can't seem to get enough of it. And so he wakes up at the break of day just as worn-out as when he went to bed, at four in the morning. He now knows what it means to be agonizingly tired. His condition, he realizes, is comparable to an affliction.

Not even while bathing, dressing, or eating can he shuck off the compulsion to recap the phases of the moonlit minute. Whenever their eyes meet, it seems to him like a plunge. He breaks into a smile so as not to betray his fright, and she smiles back, earnestly (you might say). Not being able to endure the silence, but also at a loss for words, he indicates a sigh by slightly parting his lips—then witnesses a miracle in that Thilde returns the gesture, parting her lips the very same way. It's more than I can bear, he says without words, and she answers: me too.

Perhaps the whole point of repetitions of any kind is to reach this stage. The aching happiness he feels begs for renewal, over and over. It hardly abates after hours and days but it does become mingled with fear. Because to make it lasting it has to be amplified and expanded, and he doesn't feel capable of the initiative this would take.

Anticipation mixed with fear preoccupies him for quite some time. It gnaws at him day and night. Sometimes (when his mother calls, for instance, and he musters all his strength to make up lies) he manages to free himself for a few minutes from the mental stranglehold and, full of pity, to gaze upon his energy-consuming inner life, not exactly a bed of roses. Equanimity is preferable; it's a state he's familiar with.

Imperturbable is what he needs to be if he wants to work, which is why he's here. He opens books and forces himself to read them, breezes through them but takes in none of it, because his mind is busy with other things. He also thinks about finishing the letter to his father, but his resolution gets him nowhere. As he reads through the part he's written already and runs across the remark about not having seen the chambermaid yet, his thoughts are instantly pulled in another direction; they begin composing another letter, describing the way things really are between Thilde and Viktor. He's tempted to put his pleasure and pain into words—but he couldn't possibly address these words to his father, for they would only end up losing a good part of their truth, depicting a son who is worthy of his father: a go-getter. Frau Erika would be a more suitable recipient. He's not ashamed, he contemplates, to show his feelings and weaknesses to her. Their lapse in correspondence has been due to his own reluctance to write; his desire to write will revive it. He fishes out the last two unanswered rose letters and puts himself in the mood by reading them. The required Erika style sets in. His pen is not yet in hand when already a flower of speech begins to bloom: the eye's arrow which opens wounds that only love can heal.

His letter goes on and on. The urge to unload his burden onto someone else is great, and Frau Erika's preformed rose idiom makes it easy to find the right expression. Figures of speech like "interchange of souls," "moon's unclouded majesty," or "beams of coming tenderness" roll off the tip of his pen. Even the sun is invoked (its kiss the source of Viktor's bliss), despite it being nighttime. The curious thing is that Viktor, who means to dispel reality through writing, ends up in regions where reality and dream can no longer be kept apart, where desire takes shape (on paper) and the story's dynamic prevails over the facts. Is this because he's learned to see the things of this world not as static but as progressive, where being means becoming and the oak is in the acorn? Has his daily perusal of periodicals, which don't report on the snowdrifts but on the *removal* of snowdrifts, paid off in this respect? Or is it Frau Erika's expectations that guide his writing hand telepathically? In any case, the kind of honey Frau Erika hopes to suck out of Viktor's letters is copiously manufactured here. By anticipating later developments, he sets himself on fire. This is prospective thinking, developed into an art.

The length of his letter means one thing: that the reply he receives the very next morning is even longer. It offers him the chance to reread the culmination of his fantasies, enhanced by a description of the feelings that overwhelmed the letter's recipient. The prince (now referred to as "her precious") is asked to reveal even more of these tidbits. He obliges her request and dreams for days, looks for rhymes, writes; he waits for a reply, indulges her insistent appeals for more kiss-and-tell disclosures—until one afternoon his dreams are cut short. Reality announces itself with a rap on the door. It stands in the doorway, huge and hairy. The dreamer is asked without a whiff of pleasantry to put on his coat and step outside. "You and I," says Sebastian, "need to have a chat, but not here."

THE DUEL

To scrawny Viktor, the most menacing thing about mighty Sebastian is his silence. His every attempt to break it with questions or chitchat is thwarted. Viktor can hardly keep up with the giant's footsteps. He soon begins to sweat—from exertion as well as fear.

A sunny day is expiring. It was thawing in the afternoon, but now that the sun is gone, it's freezing again and Dead Man's Road is iced over. Viktor often slips, grabs on to Sebastian, and asks him to slow down. The answer to his repeated question: Why the excursion if they just need to have a talk? is forthcoming once they reach the cemetery. The house no longer visible behind the trees, Sebastian comes to a stop and finally breaks his silence. With a calm betraying considerable restraint, he asks if Viktor doesn't agree that the two of them are in each other's way.

Although Viktor had suspected the reason for their tête-à-tête, he's startled to have his suspicions confirmed. Fear has oftentimes prevented him from preparing himself mentally; now it impairs his thinking entirely, weakens his knees, and makes his voice tremble as he asks, How come? and Why? and then claims to not even know which third person, left unnamed, Sebastian is even talking about.

It's not a good strategy. He chose it without a second thought. Instead of forcing the prickly giant to listen, dispelling his suspicion, or inducing him to speechify like usual and thereby channeling off his aggression, Viktor's refusal to face the facts only succeeds in enraging him even more and, words having failed, provokes him to use his fists.

The punch lands on Viktor's cheek, below his left eye. The pain it causes is minimal because it encounters little resistance: Viktor goes down while the fist is still flying. He lies in the snow, trying his best to look dead, and considers, once his faculties are restored, not only the mistakes he's made but also the possibilities of setting them straight. Sebastian, who's startled by the effect of his blow, can't decide at first whether to resume his question-and-answer session, carry on with the violence, leave the scene of the crime, or offer his help, which gives Viktor plenty of time to think things over. From what he could gather from Sebastian's questions and the threatening gestures accompanying them, the giant thinks he's been deceived, undoubtedly due to misinformation (alas, Frau Erika is to blame) prefiguring the developments desired by Viktor, so that the obvious thing would be to rectify the error, Sebastian having put himself in the wrong because of it, and explain to him what really happened, which is to say, nothing at all. But the idea is quickly discarded, because Viktor keeps on thinking. The smarting in his cheek has by no means deadened the feelings that have stirred him now for weeks; brute force hasn't stifled his hopes. Having already dreamed himself into his romantic future in his letter writing, it's not hard for him to make the leap and treat the conceivable as a foregone conclusion —in other words, to feel the reality of what Sebastian takes as a given, to suffer the blow as punishment for what is bound to happen anyway. This is the standpoint he'll take, or so he resolves, in answering the question that's been put to him three times already and which three times he's dodged under the pretext of not knowing what to make of it. What's more, he'll answer it in such a way that Sebastian's conviction of having moral right on his side will begin to falter.

For the time being, Viktor is still lying low in the snow, playing dead. He endeavors to breathe unnoticeably and does not even move when Sebastian—at first angry, then imploring—tells him to say something. But he doesn't torment his perpetrator for long. Signs of life appear as Sebastian crouches down next to him, slips off his victim's glove, and tries to feel his pulse. Viktor strains to open his eyes, indicates with a painful smile how embarrassed he is of his own weakness, and finally tries to get up, supported by Sebastian. Faintly groaning, he fingers his wounded cheek, sensing with satisfaction that it's swollen. He squints his left eye to accentuate the impression of being disabled and looks around for a tree to lean on. He limps the two-yard stretch to the tree but realizes he's overdoing it. Sebastian's face displays distrust. Looking to appease him, Viktor says, "Sorry, I've been acting foolishly," which doesn't have the desired effect. While it's true that Sebastian says "Me too," it doesn't sound very conciliatory. Viktor is therefore feeling uneasy when the fist-swinger approaches again.

The passing thought that the tree he's leaning on would easily lend itself as a martyr's stake eventually gets Viktor moving. He insists on going back to the house on the pretext that he's freezing. He'd like to be within eyeshot of New Glory again, fast. It's comforting to be allowed to hang on Sebastian's arm. Having the giant next to him is better than face-to-face.

But this relative security does not last long. No sooner have they left the trees behind (it was almost dark beneath them) and headed toward an illuminated New Glory than Sebastian frees himself from Viktor, plants himself squarely in front of him, and repeats for the fourth time (he calls it the last time) the question Viktor now knows how to answer but which he doesn't answer just yet, because he considers it more impressive to have what's supposed to sound like the bitter truth be preceded by inner struggle. He gives the impression of being momentarily startled, dodges Sebastian's gaze, puckers his forehead, and contracts his eyebrows above his nose. He lays his hand on his swollen cheek as if there were a pain that needed easing, then, obeying a sudden impulse, lifts his stare and looks Sebastian in the eye without flinching. His soft-spoken, almost meek reply has nothing to do with fear; it's meant to indicate that he knows how much it will pain the questioner.

If this is the case, you wouldn't know it by reading Sebastian's face, which, we know already, is disguised behind a beard. The real proof is the fact that this otherwise voluble man is suddenly speechless. At first he says nothing at all, and then no more than "Aha!" before hurriedly heading back alone. Viktor follows him at a leisurely

120

pace. He has two reasons to be satisfied with himself. First, he really did tell the truth, as he later attests to repeatedly. Second, he's quite certain that the brief dialogue on Dead Man's Road, consisting of the question, What do you want from her? and the answer, I want to marry her! will sooner or later reach his intended.

By the Way

Viktor's valor during the snow blockade has secured him a special status for all time. The rooms normally off-limits to guests are open to him in the future. If by some odd chance he misses a meal, he can either help himself in the kitchen or Olga will prepare him a special dish, generally with loving attention. And no one disputes his place at the kitchen table, across from Thilde, as life at the home returns to normal. That he gives it up anyway in exchange for the seat at his old guest table in the dining room has not only to do with his coworkers, who've just arrived and should not be given too clear a view of his lifestyle; he's also fleeing from Sebastian.

Sebastian's behavior makes every meal an ordeal. Viktor is sometimes concerned about him, sometimes downright scared of him. Sometimes he pities Thilde, sometimes Sebastian, then it's himself he feels sorry for. Since he's never learned from personal experience what jealousy is, he can't understand Sebastian's lack of self-control, the chip on his shoulder, his despondency, and his sudden fits of crude hilarity. He's particularly appalled by the blindness, the unpredictability, the lack of any design he could adapt himself to. Just what, he wonders, does a man who fancies he's been deceived get out of picking a quarrel with his supposedly successful rival over some minor detail (where the empty beer bottles go, for example)? What does he stand to gain by exposing Viktor's secret affair with Thilde, by making crass allusions and villainizing Thilde, or by fixing Viktor with a menacing stare from soup to dessert without so much as uttering a word; or by bursting into laughter at breakfast at the boneheads who believe in constancy of character, because it serves them right for being deceived when they turn their backs for a second? Why does he make a fool of himself by claiming, now that the worst of winter has passed, that it's too cold in his room and that he is moving downstairs into the room next to Viktor's? And how does all this unpleasantness, which can only work to his disadvantage in Thilde's eyes, square off with the fact that Sebastian, who never wasted a thought on Tita before, is now all of a sudden concerned about her welfare and, whenever Thilde's and Olga's (of course unsuccessful) attempts to get her into a nursing home are mentioned, condemns her being "put into barracks," as he calls it, and this in the most emphatic terms?

Not wanting to spoil his appetite from anxiety, and eager to avoid any unpleasant encounters with the jealous man, Viktor withdraws to the guest dining room. Granted, he misses the sight of Thilde, but at least he can eat his meals in peace. His tablemate, a secretary by the name of Buhse, doesn't molest him with conversation; her respect for Herr Kösling Junior is too great, and her two school-age sons, all but immune to good manners, constantly have to be kept in line. Viktor, then, has time to think while eating. He's not concerned about Sebastian's ranting (which only serves to discredit himself), but he is concerned about Sebastian's intercession on behalf of Tita. Because a wavering Thilde is willing to listen.

Sebastian is right in perceiving that no one stands in the way of their burgeoning happiness more than Tita. Her condition has rapidly worsened since her abortive excursion to Poland. She's seldom clear-headed, and this, too, could be feigned. Her inner chaos is masked by discipline, especially when strangers are around. She greets them and tells them to pull up a chair, even smiles and says, "Fine, thank you!"; she joins the conversation with phrases like "Time sure flies!" or "What must be, must be!" and looks attentive when spoken to. It's only when she asks about the kids her conversation partner doesn't have do you notice that she's rattling off set phrases, that nothing more than a mechanism of good breeding is concealing her innermost thoughts and feelings from strangers. Once the strangers are gone, the mechanism stops working. She's then hounded by a restless urge, without any apparent rhyme or reason. A fear that can't be verbalized drives her sometimes to flee, sometimes to seek out Thilde, who then can't leave her alone for a minute, and yet at other times into an alcohol-induced stupor. She steals the booze from Max's supplies or bribes Thomas to steal it for her. But when she offers him two hundred marks for a bottle, his conscience is pricked and he blows the whistle. Thilde, who's been suffering sleepless nights without complaint, bursts into tears when she finds out about it. She says to Viktor, who stands by helplessly, "Sometimes I wish she were dead."

Viktor only wishes she were in a nursing home. And since his wish is fervent, he does something to speed it along. In the next phone call with his mother, he prefaces his appeal with "By the way" (which is intended to ease the burden of what is for him a rather weighty issue). He tries to make Agnola believe that the connection to him and his dissertation is only secondary, that human suffering experienced close up obviously arouses his compassion and therefore hinders his work.

Despite the fact that he delivers his report on Tita (whom he always refers to as the old lady) in the blithely derisive tone he learned from his mother, he has reason to doubt his indifference is credible. For no sooner has he put forward his request to obtain for Tita one of the few available beds in a nursing home than his mother brings up the individual he took pains to leave out of their conversation: Klothilde, whose name she of course finds comical, and which to him has long ago ceased to be funny. "Looks like Klothilde," she says, "has got her hands full with the old bag after all."

Viktor now changes his tone. Instead of being derisive, which didn't have the desired effect, he tries to be matter-of-fact about it, referring not merely to Klothilde but to Klothilde Lüderitz. She really can't be blamed, he says, for wanting to live her own life; after all, she's a nurse, he only recently learned, and not a chambermaid, so it's only logical, the way he sees it, that she longs to return to her actual profession.

Viktor doesn't find out if an unknown girl and her longing to return to her original occupation can in fact prompt Agnola to take action, because when she hears the word *hospital* she immediately thinks of J.K. and is compelled to give a detailed report of his slow but steady recovery. But Viktor is positive his mother won't let him down. And since his father's illness doesn't interest him at the moment, he pictures himself, while still on the phone, handing Klothilde Lüderitz the necessary documents, and her, in a transport of joy, taking him in her arms.

The Proposal

If our readers are only briefly informed, or even left in the dark about the many events of the coming (and surprisingly fleeting) winter weeks, then this is to put them in Viktor's shoes. Because Viktor is becoming increasingly unable to take in anything not directly affecting his plans. The radio, television, and newspaper reports brought to him from around the world are heard, viewed, and read only to be forgotten in short order. But even the events in his immediate surroundings scarcely move him, including the ones that demand his attention. A budget commission from the Ministry, which spends a whole day inspecting the books, rooms, and staff and promises upon leaving to send a replacement for Max, sends everyone into a frenzy—everyone, that is, except Viktor. The day Olga pays her first visit to the prison where Max is being held and afterward refers to him as a bastard only sticks in his mind because Thilde prepares the meals that day and puts up with him in the kitchen. When policemen come to register Max's cars, engines, and spare parts, Viktor is there, physically, with Püppi on his arm, but his thoughts are elsewhere, contemplating a sentence Thilde uttered which, he assumes, was intended to imply that the gardener has no right to carry on acting jealous. He doesn't even notice that the cows are sold and carted off. He avoids contact with the other guests (mostly married couples with children spending their vacation at the rest home), Frau Buhse included, who shyly let on to him that all she needs is a father for her two sons. He uses his work as an excuse, and it does in fact take up some of his time, because he has to learn at least enough material to be able to speak plausibly about the progress he's making when his phone-happy mother rings him up.

Alas, Sebastian is ever present on Viktor's limited horizon. He really has moved in next door to Viktor, and although he stays out of Viktor's way and doesn't deliberately make noise, his proximity makes Viktor uneasy. He's forced to hear every noise next door, has to try to guess what Sebastian is up to, and can never get away from the idea that every step he takes is being monitored. Because there can only be one reason for his moving downstairs: the jealous man has assigned himself the role of watchman.

One evening, when Viktor is sitting at his desk listening to the quiet next door instead of working, asking himself whether Sebastian is sleeping or eavesdropping, a knock at the door announces a visit. It's Olga. She looks around unabashedly, sits down, lights up, and says twice that it's time she paid him a visit, before lapsing into silence so that Viktor is forced to speak. The best he comes up with is the unchanging and peaceful winter weather, which he says is healthy, but which doesn't interest Olga one bit. She stares at him fixedly and doesn't say a word. Viktor tries the topic of Püppi, likewise to no avail. Only after she's smoked her third cigarette and Viktor has wrapped up his fourth conversation starter do her slender lips give away what she's been thinking about all along: her autobiography, which Viktor, of course, has heard before.

The hope her opening sentence awakens in Viktor—"You know my life already"—goes unfulfilled. Without taking her eyes off him, she overlooks his eager nods, ignores his comment "You told me that already," and finds neither an ordering principle nor an end to her story. She talks slowly (due to her slightly palsied tongue) but also in a quiet, montonous tone; the effect is all but soporific. Viktor barely listens—until the moment the name Thilde bursts forth between scraps of memory, at which point he's all ears. He tries to bring some order into the narrative chaos, tries to put back together what Olga tears apart, and soon realizes that whenever the name Thilde crops up it's intended as a comparison. She doesn't mean to say anything bad about her, Olga repeatedly points out, but she can't help it. She, Olga, the daughter of a good family, who even learned piano, has no choice but to call the girl's parentage dark and obscure, her culinary skills (compared with her own) modest, her character poor. Stuck-up is how Olga describes her while boastfully describing herself as modest. Besides, she's too young; a woman needs experience, and she, Olga, has plenty of that, without being too old either: "Because what difference do a couple of lousy years make!"

Viktor's urge to have a drink, which gives him a reason to pull out a bottle, is only a pretext; he thinks it might do Olga well to have another. But she turns his offer down; schnapps, she says, doesn't agree with her. Her eyes repeatedly wander though, away from Viktor and toward the bottle, as she resumes her story. And when she again brings up her parental home—a house with books, no less—and Viktor pours himself a third drink, she finally reaches for her glass, and then hangs on to the bottle.

Her tippling has no effect on her behavior or speech. Viktor, on the other hand, who's long since forgotten that Sebastian might be eavesdropping next door, is mellowed by the alcohol. It dissipates his shock at her proposal, gradually turning it into sympathy. The misunderstanding on which her line of thinking is based he finds endearing, the way she presents the matter, irreproachably decent—because she asks him nothing, doesn't force an answer out of him and offers him the possibility of not understanding her chaotic ramblings.

She assumes that a man his age who is not yet a husband has no greater desire than to become one and is therefore keen on single women—which in the close-knit community of New Glory means Thilde, however unfit she may be as a spouse. Now, if this callow young man who, as Olga sees it, isn't looking for a wife who's a child but a wife who can be a mother to him, if this fellow, in his blindness, hasn't noticed that the pool of eligible brides has recently gotten bigger, well, then, it's up to her to call his attention to it. She'd often thought about it before but only found the courage to speak up when her anxiety about the future was added to the equation.

"It's over with me and New Glory," she says, "my time is up here." Max has taken his revenge: he blew the whistle on her and reported her to the hygiene department. They were here the other day, unnoticed by Viktor, two women who knew about everything thanks to

Max, her smoking while cooking, for example. She couldn't deny the accusations. Now she's no longer wanted here. They already found a new job for her, not as a cook but helping out in an industrial kitchen on the Oder, at the end of the world as far as she's concerned. Before she heads out, she thought she'd ask Viktor if he maybe needs her. She's adaptable, knows what's proper, and can do just about anything. "As a woman, I mean."

"It doesn't hurt to ask," she says, without asking. And Viktor, who before the schnapps was sure that he would accept her offer to not understand and refrain from answering, is so impressed, now that the bottle is empty, by this woman who sees her partner problems from a strictly practical point of view that he can't let her go without some kind of hope. Repressing a strong urge to say yes, he answers her the same way she posed the question: chaotically autobiographical. If she isn't too far gone already, she can gather from his memories of father, mother, and girls that her assessment of him was right—he just needs some time to think it over. She can buy that, and heads to the door with rigid, groping steps, refusing his escort. "No hard feelings," is her closing remark, and Viktor, who does not have the capacity left for mental exertion of any great magnitude, is left pondering her figure of speech.

THE BLESSED MOTHER

More impressive than the institution's quietude and cleanliness is the crucified Jesus welcoming all who enter. He's hanging nearly life-size next to the unoccupied porter's office, reminding Viktor that he's on foreign ground, that he is wholly unfamiliar with the order and customs here. Thilde is intimidated too, not daring to raise her voice above a whisper. Only Tita is lacking respect. She weaves through the pillars with a heavy step, finds the round arches old-fashioned, calls up the stairs, "Anybody home?" then plops down on the steps. After a while she inquires, "What are we doing here, anyway?"

Viktor ventures further. He knocks on doors, behind which nothing stirs; he goes through the back door into the park but only sees snow and hanging laundry. At last, he yanks open a giant portal, which he takes for a passageway, and is frightened by a host of indignant stares: he's landed himself in the chapel, where all of the residents are busy praying.

It's no great chore for him to wait, as long as Thilde's at his side. Just looking at her would be pastime enough; now he even gets to whisper in her ear. They sit on the stone steps next to Tita, who's tuckered out from the long bus and train rides, while Thilde explains to Viktor her double-edged fear: that the nuns will end up rejecting Tita and, then again, that they'll keep her here. In other words, Thilde is unsure of her decision and wants Viktor to support it.

He's glad to do so. He goes through the list of reasons he's often cited before, summarizing them with the assertion that everyone has the right to live their own life. He even goes so far as to express his own desire to spend his waning days in a place like this, then quotes his mother, who in contacting the people whose influence extends to Catholic circles, said, "The roof we provide for our aging loved ones cannot be Christian enough."

Viktor is regurgitating another one of his mother's bromides—that the sisters' work is their calling—when one of them appears behind him. She introduces herself as Sister Benedikte, a woman whose height and nimbleness make her seem less stout than she is.

Viktor isn't sure if the proper reply to "*Grüss Gott!*"—"God greet you!"—is its repetition. He tries it out but can't tell by the sister's face, which is smooth and pure like the coif that surrounds it, if he's struck the right chord. He also doesn't figure out if it's correct to give her a hearty handshake. But there is no misunderstanding her reaction when Viktor tells her they've come because of Frau Lüderitz, who's been admitted here by the Episcopal Ordinariate. With a voice attuned to the hard of hearing, Sister Benedikte says nobody but her admits anyone here.

They're invited to sit down, in a room that is half administrative, half doctor's office, Thilde and Viktor on stools, Tita in a wingback chair. Cane between her legs, Tita sits stiffly on the edge of her chair as though she's about to get up and leave. But she is attentive. And when she's asked a question, she knows how to answer, fairly appropriately even: "Thanks, I can't complain" or "Well, I'm no spring chicken."

Thilde tried for days to prepare Tita for this interview. She went into detail about the advantages of living in a home, practiced the anticipated discussion with her, and gave her strict orders on the ride there to be friendly, listen well, and answer clearly. Now she sees it was all for naught, that although Tita is behaving properly, she doesn't understand what's going on. Thilde therefore tries to answer for Tita, but Sister Benedikte won't let her. As she said on the phone already, the home is understaffed, meaning they can't afford to take in invalids.

Sister Benedikte does not like having new arrivals ordained from above, but she does like Tita. She's got her down for a straight-talking woman, as she puts it, because when asked if she's happy to come to the home, Tita answered, "No use complaining!"

Sister Benedikte vents her spleen on the young people. Taking them for a married couple, she accuses them of all the crimes the modern world, obsessed as it is with utility, is committing against the elderly. Instead of being respected, the elderly are held in contempt. They're unable to work anymore and no one wants their advice either because their store of experience has aged faster than they have. They get shoved aside for standing in the way of progress. If bread were scarce, they wouldn't be given any, but since it's time for love and kindness that people are short on nowadays, they save on that instead. "Mind you," says Sister Benedikte, "depriving someone of love and affection can be just as lethal."

With Thilde unable to speak on account of her tears, Viktor senses that it's his duty to step in and placate the furious nun. He nods considerately at what she is saying, tossing in an occasional Yes, you're right on that count. He and his wife are greatly attached to her grandma (whose housekeeping skills, by the way, would certainly be a welcome addition here, considering how fit and active she is) and would never let her go if he (being a diplomat) didn't have to go abroad for several years. In other words, they're forced to find a new home for her, but it has to be one where love reigns. "That's why we came to you," Viktor closes, but looks past Sister Benedikte as he says it, at a picture hanging behind her. It's a color print in a golden frame; in front of a sweeping landscape of meadows, woods, villages, mountains, and castles, under a sky that isn't blue but yellow, a Madonna stands, young and resplendent, in a long, flowing, emerald cloak, her open, outstretched arms spreading the crimson cape on her narrow shoulders so that the assortment of people below, helpless and small as dwarves, can hide beneath it: the beggar and the pope, the peasant and the queen, the knight and the maid.

Viktor knows how to convey the fascination the picture exerts on him, so much so that Sister Benedikte reverently keeps silent so as not to disturb him. She shifts in her seat to see him better when he steps up to the picture. Yes, he mutters after a long pause, as if to himself, that's just the way he pictured it; he's altogether ignorant in these matters, of course, and yet this is a symbol that speaks to him immediately—no, more than that, it touches him, powerfully even, if you can say that about such tenderness.

You can tell that Sister Benedikte is proud of the effect her Madonna has. She walks over to Viktor and explains to him the particulars, even from an art history perspective, but is quick to add that it's not about aesthetics: the painting is not hanging here because of its beauty, it's here because of its truth, as both a solace and an incentive. Viktor wags his head, voices the assumption that the painter must have been a very devout individual, and when he comes up with the expression "crowned goodness," senses that victory is near. Sister Benedikte, who's burning to show Viktor more pictures, asks the ladies to come along; they'll be passing Tita's future home on the way. Provided the doctor, who won't be here for another two days, gives his okay, Sister Benedikte will try admitting Tita—"on a trial basis," she emphasizes. Frau Helwig, alone in her room since Frau Paalzow went to meet to her Maker, should be thrilled to have some company.

If Sister Benedikte is right about this last bit, then Frau Helwig, sitting on a stool crocheting, sure knows how to hide her joy. She doesn't return a single greeting, listens to Sister Benedikte's explanations with a hostile expression, eyes Tita from top to toe, then carries on with her needlework. "She's a suspicious one, Granny Helwig," Sister Benedikte chirps, and cuts short her instructions regarding the schedule of masses, linens, and house rules because Viktor has immersed himself in another painting and can't quite figure out the symbolism behind its portrayal of footwear. Sister Benedikte tells him (in a zealous tone) about Saint Hedwig, who went barefoot to the lepers in order to be their equals, and is distracted from paying attention to Tita, who paces back and forth nervously, rubs her chin, and mumbles, "Is it worth it?" among other malapropisms.

The qualification "Only on a trial basis!" is repeated twice, followed by a hearty farewell. Frau Helwig is coaxed into putting down her pot holders and holding out her hand to Viktor. Viktor gives Tita a hug, but Sister Benedikte insists on seeing the young people to the door. "You and I," she says to Tita, "will wave good-bye to them."

However, nothing comes of it. After Viktor's thank-you speech, which doesn't fail to mention the Madonna of the Protective Mantle, Tita bids good-bye as well. "It was a pleasure," she says to Sister Benedikte and is the first to head out the door. Viktor, who is suddenly seized with anger, manages to conceal it behind a smile but cannot help applying a steely grip, hauling Tita back in. "Ouch! You're hurting me!" Tita yells at him, then willingly obeys Thilde, who declares with tender gruffness that she's sending her straight to bed.

Viktor doesn't follow them back in. He waits instead under the crucifix across from the porter's office. The last he hears is Tita's question—when are they going to get her out of this hospital—and Sister Benedikte's response: "Oh dear!"

I Do

The small rural town in the Mark Brandenburg where the nuns from Silesia, Sisters of Mercy of St. Borromeo, have run their old-age home since the end of the war must be seen here (however unjust) through Thilde's eyes, because the gloom that unexpectedly besets her in the hours to come is not wholly unrelated to it. Rather than mention it by name, which would be tantamount to its character assassination, the remark of an elderly inhabitant, offered in reply to a comment of Viktor's in which the word *wasteland* came up, should suffice to explain why it is the way it is: "You should have seen it in '45!" The town, that is, which because of its strategic value lost everything else along with it—that is to say, was flattened.

Well, it's not flat anymore. Over the years, civic leaders with a love of order have turned it into a concrete jungle: neatly arranged, rectangular and gray. A straight thoroughfare on the scale of a freeway divides the town in two. Five-story prefab apartment blocks line the road, blocking from view the old backstreets with their dilapidated houses and a wasteland of garages, wooden sheds, and weed-infested concrete structures. A giant square spreads out where the old town center used to be, dwarfing a kiosk and a row of parked cars. Red banners and the yellow plastic sheeting forming a roof over the bus station fail to break the monotony of gray, tending rather to accentuate it. The sidewalks are cramped by walls of dirty snow.

Viktor and Thilde have to cross the street to reach the train station but are held up by a long military convoy. The noise prohibits conversation. It doesn't prevent them from exchanging glances, but these are few and far between because Thilde is not in the mood. When she does glance back at Viktor, whose eyes are constantly trained on her, there is nothing loving about it; it's an expression that Viktor takes as signifying sorrow, fear, or distress, until she explains to him (much, much later) that it was actually a look of reproach! If it weren't for him, her look is meant to say, she never would have had to hurt Tita like this.

Since Viktor is not yet aware of this explanation (which gives him what he wants, in a roundabout way), his disappointment is great. He'd pictured it differently, their return trip after a deed well done: full of joy for what they'd accomplished, full of thankfulness for him who made it possible, full of happiness at being released from years of burden. Instead of the sigh of relief he imagined (alone at last!), all he hears, once the roar of engines passes and he's able to hear again, are her worries about Tita. Of all the things Viktor had hoped for from the trip back, only one of them is fulfilled: they've missed the afternoon train. Hence Viktor proposes, as though it had only just occurred to him, that they spend the night at a hotel. After all, if they took the evening train they would not arrive at New Glory till three in the morning, but if they stay in town and get up early, they might be able to check on Tita before they leave.

That the only hotel in town is located right at the train station puts a damper on his dream-wish. The restaurant, where they learn that every room is taken, is occupied by soldiers. Thilde, who's greeted with cheers upon entering, wheels around and walks back out. The other tavern in town is closed for alterations, the gloomy waiting room at the train station scares them off, and the almost empty coffeehouse is closing along with the shops. Having twice walked the well-lit and nearly deserted main street from the first streetlamp to the last, they still have another three and a half hours until departure time.

Moonlight entices them to leave the center and head for the woods and fields. But whichever way they turn, all they encounter is bleakness. A kilometer-wide belt of junk and scrap yards, of warehouses, stalls and silos, and of landfills and factories surrounds the city. Army barracks on either side of the street seem to never end; concrete walls with watchtowers are joined by barbed-wire fences. This is where, insisting they turn back, Thilde finally starts to talk.

The image of her inner self that she awkwardly started one stove-side morning (how long ago it was!) she now begins to paint more vividly. She's prepared herself for it, collected facts, looked for words, and now has more to talk about than her yearnings to travel and bake. She calls her life, which she compares with being in barracks, dismal and her work meaningless, complains, when Viktor helps by asking questions, about the fact that she's never alone, that she can never pick the people she'd like to have around her. She talks, haltingly, about her mother: she's only ever heard bad things about her but she sometimes envies her negligence. She even brings up Sebastian: she can't live with him, because he's only interested in himself and not in her, because she can never say what *she* thinks, and because the personal hell she wants to escape from (New Glory) seems to him like paradise, a place he wouldn't dream of leaving.

It is always impressive when a girl has the opportunity to unburden her soul for the very first time. To Viktor, who has such a girl on his arm right now and can't seem to take his eyes off her, it's impressive to the utmost degree. He no longer notices her lisp; her ignorance of German grammar, which only occasionally manifests itself, gives her confession a lively and original note; and when he bears in mind that he and he alone is responsible for her sudden display of trust in him, thanks to his didactic skills and persistence, his sense of triumph is so great that he finds it hard being confined to the role of listener. He'd like to repay her trust with his own. Thus, whenever Thilde's account becomes too wordy, strays off course, or falters, he's busy in his mind preparing a story of his own.

The story line he works on is a life no less sad than the one he is listening to right now: because it lacks the shackles of a Tita to love and be loved by; because his parents may be there physically but never emotionally; and because a certain Flora (whom he portrays as Sebastian's counterpart) is looking for something in him that she doesn't find. Thilde, on the other hand (this is what he wants to tell her, albeit indirectly), will find in Viktor just what she needs—and he's not lying either, because he has a remarkable ability to become the person that others want him to be. To meet their expectations all he needs is to be aware of these; once he knows what they want, it doesn't take long for him to become what he's supposed to be.

But for now he's condemned to silence, because Thilde, who always kept her mouth shut around Sebastian, is making up for the missed opportunities to speak her mind. She talks more self-assuredly now, more fluently, and sometimes hastily, even though she has plenty of time. Viktor, who no longer needs to prod her with encouraging questions, is happy to hear it at first. But as time wears on, and Thilde talks for hours without even mentioning his name, he becomes a little uneasy. Something tells him the time has come to finally pop the question. But he doesn't have the nerve to do it. Never one to be decisive, he thought he could do it now, but, alas, his hopes are mistaken. All of this oppresses him, though not for long. For Thilde, as if sensing his burden, promptly takes the weight off his shoulders.

They've walked the length and breadth of the town with vigorous strides, lost their way in a garden colony, and, once they reach the street again, are standing unexpectedly in front of the Catholic old-age home, where everything is sleeping. Thilde interrupts her story about the day her mother crossed the border—who knows where—illegally, stops and stares at Viktor with the above-mentioned look of reproach (which she now explains to him), then, as though she had years of experience dealing with him, poses a question he needs only answer to finally relieve the tension they've both been under for weeks. She asks him if he still plans to carry out what he told Sebastian after their abortive duel at the cemetery, and when Viktor says, "I do," she says, "Then everything is fine."

NIGHT RIDE

Train rides are a rare experience for Viktor and his ilk. (The one he's on now is thanks to the district police, who confiscated all the motor vehicles at New Glory as a precautionary measure.) He'd not been able to appreciate the journey there because of Tita, which makes the ride back, blithely referred to as their engagement trip, all the more enjoyable. The cushy warmth of their moderately full compartment, the flickering overhead light, the clacking wheels, and the villages slumbering in moonlit fields rolling by outside the window are only sideshows to the main attraction—each other—but they're so inextricably linked that, thinking back on it later on, the one is inconceivable without the other. Their new solidarity, trying to affirm its reality through words and caresses, turns every whistle of the locomotive and every ivy-clad redbrick station building into an event. Even the drowsiness that sets in serves only to heighten the magic. The leisurely, jerky ride feels too short regardless of how long it lasts. By the time they reach their transfer point, future and present have been roughly sketched. The past still needs to be tackled.

They do this on the bus. In order to explain that the point they've arrived at is the climax, they have to retrace the path leading up to it. Their fathers have to be mentioned (Viktor's domineering, Thilde's nonexistent), their mothers (one of them ever present on the phone, the other gone missing), their teachers, professors, and senior physicians, friends, first kisses, and greatest fears. So engrossed are the two of them in their exchange of experiences, the giving being sweeter

139

than receiving, that the driver, whose only other passengers are another pair of lovers, has to announce the stop in Görtz, which is as far as they paid to go.

Of course, the mass of memories that wants to be shared is hardly spent by the time they get off, and the short walk down Dead Man's Road isn't long enough either. There's an urgent need to keep on talking once they're home. Viktor has just learned that Sebastian is history, and Thilde now knows that because of her a dissertation has not been written. This loads them with responsibility which they'll have to help each other bear. Neither food nor sleep nor light is required. All they need is to be left alone.

But this is a luxury they won't be granted. No sooner have their eyes adjusted to the darkness of Thilde's room than it is suddenly illuminated. The light that casts their shadows onto the wall comes from outside. Only now do they hear the sound of an engine. A truck is approaching the house. Someone gets out. While the truck is turning around, its headlights conjuring in the window frame the black-and-white image of a winter landscape complete with plum-tree skeletons, someone hammers away at the door. "Doggone it," cries Tita, "isn't anybody home around here?"

Viktor hardly sleeps at all despite spending the night alone in his room. Fantasies of murder preoccupy him. He pictures himself sitting on Tita's bed, pressing her with friendly insistence to have a glass of water; she complains of its bitter taste but drinks it up obediently.

Castles and Gardens

Agnola, who loves to entertain and have people over, only invites a handful to her birthday: close friends with whom she can mourn, as she puts it, because a day that reminds you how old you are is no cause for celebration. Viktor's presence has always been mandatory. What better proof, then, of the respect she has for the cloistered existence and work routine of her son than the fact that this year she relieves him of his obligation to visit. "If you were already in Switzerland, or Australia for all I care," she playfully says on the phone, "I'd force you to make a lightning visit. But I wouldn't want you to have to leave your Prussian wasteland. You might get it in your head never to go back, and that's a risk I'd rather not take." Viktor is happy at first to gain an extra day but later decides not to accept his mother's sacrifice after all. "We want to make things clear right from the start," he says to Thilde in a sudden fit of rebelliousness, and on the evening before the party, he wires to Potsdam not his birthday greetings but the announcement that the greetings will be extended in person: by him and his fiancée.

Thilde has to take the day off at New Glory. The reason they give is their search for a nursing home for Tita—which is not wholly untrue, because another reason for their visit is to convince Agnola to obtain the referral slip they need. The telephone calls Viktor made on behalf of Thilde led to the discovery that nursing homes, too, are in short supply, and that waiting times of a year or more are altogether common.

Viktor, well aware since childhood that people come from around the world to visit the castles and gardens of his native city, is surprised to find that Thilde has never seen them before. He's happy to be able to show them to her, but the pavilions and palaces covered with an even layer of snow, the leafless trees and bushes, the dried-up fountains and boarded-up statues awaiting a warmer season only bore her. Viktor stands freezing in front of Sanssouci, telling her all he knows about Frederick II and his successors (it's not much), but Thilde just wants to see the shops. The stuffy air of a department store finally brings her to life. Every stall has to be inspected, even the toy and sports department arouses her interest. The purchase of a dressing gown that Tita will soon need in the nursing home keeps her occupied for hours. Then, sitting in a café, the last stop before their final destination, Viktor begins recounting a childhood memory that came back to him in the park, and she suddenly remembers the blouse she couldn't decide to buy. She asks him to stay put, runs back to the department store, and moments later stands radiant with joy, holding up her new purchase to Viktor, who couldn't care less. And yet she didn't forget his childhood memory, she asks him to continue where he left off: "Your father, you were saying, sent you to boxing lessons to toughen you up, but you played hooky—what happened then?" And Viktor, who has to suppress his urge to correct his bride's pronunciation of the word *blouse*, likewise suppresses the comment, *Your shopping lust seems stronger than your interest in me!* and resumes his story about his refusal to box. The story makes Thilde fearful of Agnola. Because a child, she explains, who, first of all, can't rid himself of the murderous thought that he's at the mercy of those who want to make him robust, who, second of all, spends every Tuesday afternoon during the winter months slinking around palaces and gardens, wet and freezing, just waiting to be seen and denounced by friends, and who, in the third place, as an eleven-year-old well knows that his guilty lies and refusal to obey orders will have to be exposed sooner or later—a child like that, living in fear day and night for months on end, says Thilde, has already been punished enough. A good beating, doled out in an initial fury, regretted and forgotten in a matter of minutes—she could understand that, but not the agreement his parents reached, which she calls a conspiracy, the calculating punishment she alleges is due to lovelessness. She's willing to believe that his father, full of contempt for his pampered son, a boy so unlike himself, would come up with a method of punishment like that; but that his mother had a part in it, instead of protesting and trying to thwart it, is simply outrageous. To allow a child to keep on lying, well aware of what's going on, only to punish him more severely by exposing the offense on his birthday, a day he expects to be showered with gifts—that's downright mean in Thilde's view. And the punishment he receives she calls cruel: four weeks in isolation, not a word, not a gesture, not a glance for the little criminal, total withdrawal of love and affection. The way the child becomes desperate after his initial defiance, the way he cries and begs for attention, the way he stands in front of his parents' bedroom door at night, pleading forgiveness, only to find the door locked, and the way he eventually saves himself by coming down with an illness and fever—even after so many years it all makes Thilde furious. Viktor, having opened up to her and shared his memory in order to bring them closer, now senses that he's put a wedge between them. She interprets to their disadvantage what he says about his parents, unjustly in his opinion. Viktor defends them as best he can, but Thilde remains unimpressed. "When we have kids someday," she says, "they're going to be raised differently, whether you like it or not."

Having meanwhile left the café behind them, having passed through a city gate and reached a deserted street with villas and gardens, he not only promises her to wholly place his trust in her child-rearing instincts, but reinforces it with a hug and a kiss. He doesn't have to ask her not to bring up things like this with Agnola, because she herself says something to that effect. When, feeling cheerful again, she adds that her job is to teach him and not his mother, but instead of using the verb "to teach" she says her job is to "learn" him, he suddenly wishes she would pretend to be a mute in the hours yet to come. Of course, he wouldn't dare suggest it.

DISHWASHING

The good impression Thilde makes at the little birthday gathering might have something to do with her youth, but it definitely has something to do with her reticence. Five people more interested in talking than listening are invariably relieved by a sixth person in their midst who doesn't try to steal the spotlight. Rabid talkers don't need other rabid talkers, they need listeners; and someone who keeps quiet, asks questions, or actually answers the questions asked of her is much more preferable than a conversation partner who is only waiting for a cue to strike up a topic of his own. Herr Schulz, for instance, who heads a widely represented funeral institution, depicts the troubles he has with his local managers. They're always crying out for hardwood—it's the customers, they say, who cling to old ways—and can't get it into their heads that hardwood is needed for more important things these days. As if caskets made of fiberboard with a woodlike Melafol finish look any worse! He could tell them right now how much lighter they are than the ones made of oak. But when he tries to explain the resistance he encountered to a prize-winning suggestion for improvement—replacing the metal fittings with a lacquered wood-flour composite—he's interrupted by another guest who knows all too well about enemies concealing their true intentions under the false mantle of time-honored ways. The sculptor Max Uphues (who resists turning his name into a Greek-sounding Ufüs, but pronounces it in straightforward Low German: Up-hoos) produces busts that are truly needed, mostly of Ernst Thälmann. As plaster or bronze cast-ings, they could grace every house of culture, every pioneer palace, and every school, if it weren't for his adversaries, whom he doesn't have the opportunity to portray because Frau Belani exclaims to her husband, who is nervously cleaning his glasses, that the whole thing reminds her so much of Pfannenstiel, thereby giving Herr Belani the gambit he needs to launch into his own line of business—the fountains, bubblers, and cascades he looks after administratively and researches historically on the side. He begins with the waterworks engineer, Pfannenstiel, then moves on to cover the relation between the art of gardening at Sanssouci and capital-driven progress—un-til his wife, who only offered the opening so that she herself could claim the floor, pulls the rug out from under him, only to lose her own footing moments later—to Uphues again, who in no time goes from the Diana statue at the edge of the pool to his very own Rosa Luxemburg.

Considering that Agnola, the sovereign of the group when she doesn't happen to be in the kitchen or, like she is now, chatting away on the phone with Viktor's father—considering that Agnola has the right to interrupt anyone whenever she feels like it and to soliloquize as long as she wants, it's understandable that a guest who generally keeps quiet and has never before heard the stale old anecdotes, jokes, and reversals of fortune can easily win the sympathy of others. Thilde, who is ambitious enough (at first) to try and understand what she hears, often poses primitive questions that betray the gaps in her knowl-edge. But this doesn't dampen the storytellers' enthusiasm. Quite the contrary: her questions about burial rites, stelae, minarets, and pump chambers offer the chance to begin at the beginning and get down, way down, to the nitty-gritty. Particularly Herr Belani, who thinks he can discern that these dainty little ears, unfortunately covered by tightly combed black hair, are less keen on hearing about statues and caskets than about waterworks, is all worked up by his itch to talk. He overlooks the rule of etiquette that only one person is allowed to speak at a time, inches his chair toward Thilde, and, without giving a damn about Schulz's talk of rationalization, embarks on the story of fountains, under his breath but with all the thrilling details—that is to say, from the very beginning.

While Thilde learns that neither Baumann nor Heintze and George nor said Pfannenstiel succeeded in getting the fountain to work so that, except for the famous Good Friday in 1754 when the jet shot up once then died just as quickly, the old king never got to see how the waterworks beautified his park, Viktor is explaining to his mother how things stand with him in the present and the future—that is, he is looking for a chance to do so, but Agnola doesn't afford him the opportunity just yet. First, once his mother is done, he has to talk on the phone to his father, who praises him for making the trip to Potsdam; then, in the kitchen while whipping cream, he has to talk to his mother about his father, whose illness has changed him enormously. Unlike Agnola's housekeeper, who he now learns hasn't changed a bit: she always calls in sick when company comes. Her loving employees, on the other hand, can always be counted on to make sure that their boss's birthday is a red-letter day. Viktor sensed as soon as he got here that Agnola is loath to engage in serious conversation. Although greeting Thilde warmly, she immediately made clear to her son that she isn't about to take this relationship any more seriously than the ones before it, asking Thilde's permission, as soon as her coat is off, to call her by her first name: "You have to understand, it's what I'm used to." She also indicated that she knows more than Viktor thinks by turning down Thilde's offer to help out in the kitchen and adding lightheartedly, "Viktor and I are the cleaning crew here. You're the guest today." She even asked about Tita, promising to help find her a nursing home, before quickly dropping the subject. She did not mention Viktor's telegram.

His resolution to set the record straight is therefore made more difficult, but he doesn't give up. He thinks he knows what's on Agnola's mind: appalled by the word *fiancée* in his telegram, she made some inquiries, probably with Frau Erika; she now fears for his dissertation, for his career in general; she's also racked by jealousy this time, whether she admits it or not, because the world Thilde comes from is strange and remote to her, and because it's the first time her son has concealed an affair from her. She senses the recalcitrance in

Viktor but is too clever to let it erupt and avoids getting tangled in conversation; she surely won't be able to keep her mouth shut when Viktor explains the foolish situation he's gotten himself into, and she knows that warning him against it or opposing it would only give rise to what she's intent on averting: a quarrel that might impair the trust between them.

Viktor, who of course is keen on avoiding a confrontation himself, is all too content to play along with her artful dodging because he knows that it's sometimes easier to achieve your aims indirectly. He falls into soft tactics during coffee and cake. He mustn't present himself to Agnola as a happy man who knows his own mind; he has to come off as a doubter, looking for advice and begging for help, a conflicted man in whom emotion and reason are battling it out. He mustn't come to her with explanations; he has to come with a confession. Anguish and contrition will compel her to grant him absolution.

While her coffee-drinking guests (soon to be sipping cognac) obey orders not to mention her birthday, discussing instead the senselessness of whitewashed coffins and (at Agnola's request) the latest fashions, Viktor puts on his look of humility. If Agnola's eyes alight on him, he turns his tortured gaze to Thilde   not without noticing her Sunday dress, a dress he found hideous ever since their arrival when Agnola condemned it with a rapid glance that only Viktor discerned.

The lecture on fountains directed at Thilde still hasn't come to an end. Herr Belani has now reached the big day, October 23, 1842, on which at precisely twelve o'clock in the afternoon technology ultimately triumphed over the laws of nature in Potsdam's parks: waterworks great and small gush into the air, bubble and splash as the crowd murmurs its approval (applause is out of the question, as Herr Belani adds, because of the king's proximity).

The amusement in His Majesty's face back then is hardly reflected in Thilde's now. This is not the way she imagined a party in better circles. She expected it to be more exciting, not so tiring. She's not used to sitting still for so long, it's hard for her to stifle her yawns, and she can't always display an interest she doesn't have. When Herr Belani pulls a pencil and notepad out of his pocket to sketch the Borsig brand steam engine and its attendant system of ten-inch pipes, Thilde feigns an urgent need to relieve herself. The bathroom offers much of interest and gives her a chance to rest for a while. From there she heads to the kitchen, having heard Viktor's mother stacking dishes. To avoid going back to the room of her torment, she offers to help as a dishwasher.

Little does she know that this is just what Agnola was after—and exactly what Viktor doesn't need. He's just begun his confession with the words "You've got to help me!" and the only reason he isn't hanging on his mother right now is that there's no room in the chaotic kitchen for the tray he's carrying, with its cups and plates and remains of cake. Ignoring the protests of Agnola, Thilde begins to tidy up. She turns on taps and looks for dishwashing liquid while Viktor is ordered back to the guests. His mother stays to do the drying, a task she soon forgets entirely. Slowly pacing to and fro while smoking cigarettes from an extra-long holder, she warmly and thoroughly sounds out Thilde, whom she can only see from behind, with her ponytail and stooping shoulders. So discreet is Agnola that she doesn't even mention her son.

She only brings up Viktor (as a complicated child always in need of his mother's help) when making a comparison between Thilde's family and her own. Although her own upbringing may have been better, if you can say such a thing, it was no less inappropriate. Her petit bourgeois lifestyle back then did not go well with a Kösling, and her education, however proud she may have been of finishing high school and college, turned out to be deficient because it lacked a political foundation. It had to go sour, she can say in retrospect. In those days, however, she was full of illusions. No one's as dumb today as she was back then (at Thilde's age). She can only admire and envy young people nowadays: because happiness, which is never long-lasting, is there for the taking; because they're capable of self-awareness and therefore know where they belong and where they don't; and because they learn early on that their skills in one setting can turn out to be less important or meaningless in another. Although even today love has a mind of its own and doesn't bother with rules or barriers, it doesn't lead to the tragedies it used to—maybe because people accept the rules nowadays, based as they are on rational principles, but definitely because everything is faster these days, so that love as well is quickly fulfilled.

"Don't get me wrong," she says, stopping right behind Thilde, who doesn't turn around. "I don't mean to say it's easier for you. I just mean that I think you're more clever than I was back then." And then Agnola keeps on talking about herself, about the respect and admiration she felt and took for love, about her desire to enter social circles that none of her girlfriends had access to, about her curiosity and her delusions of omnipotence—that is, her cockamamie optimism which led her to believe that everything she lacked could be obtained, that every obstacle could be surmounted. Her belief in her own strength was so great that, even if, say, her parents had tried to leave the country illegally, she would have considered herself immune to otherwise inviolable security regulations. Nowadays her delusions seem laughable. And yet she's not laughing now; her experiences were all too painful. She didn't stand the test. She failed—and this despite the fact that the man at her side was strong, not complicated and needy like his son.

"To be perfectly honest," she says, laying her hands on the narrow shoulders of the kitchen maid, who may or may not be listening, "I have to admit that the telegram scared me into thinking you'd be another version of me. But now that I've met you, I know it's nonsense. You're more clever than me, and it's a good thing too!" She would like her mute listener to see her happiness and tries to turn her around. But Thilde won't budge. Agnola leans forward and sees tears dripping into the dishwater, says "Now, now, what's there to cry about," calls her "my child," strokes her hair, hands her a tissue, asks her what's wrong—but still can't get a single word out of her.

The birthday girl spends the last half hour of her party doing dishes while Viktor plays rummy and the weeping girl holes up in the bathroom. The taxi comes early so their parting is brief, but Thilde finds an opportunity to try and convey what's on her mind. "You're wrong," she says, even cracking a smile, "You're wrong about me and Viktor. He's not as weak as you think, and I'm not so free of illusions. You'll see."

Viktor, who hears her when she says this but doesn't comprehend, uses the long ride back to carefully debrief her about their girl-to-girl talk. A sense of uneasiness steals over him, which he hides from Thilde. He tells her not to take things so seriously, to just wipe her memory clean of everything.

Song of the Lark

Tita is only content when things are moving. She always has to be on her feet. Rest makes the restless woman ill. No matter whether it's Klein-Kietz or a nameless place she's headed to, she's always in a rush. This is why she likes riding in cars so much. "Get a move on!" she shouts to the driver.

Frau Kösling sent not only a referral, with kind regards to Thilde, but a company car as well: a large and comfy vehicle that the garrulous young man behind the wheel calls his luxury hot rod. "Grandma" he says with the strongest Berlin accent he can muster up, "is gonna feel good on her final tour."

The fields and woods are still covered in snow, but sunshine has dried up the road; only the seasonal roads have puddles. Tita is happier than she has been in a long time. She looks out the window with rapt attention, taking in the signs of spring: the villagers out and about with no hats and gloves on, the open windows of schools, and the barges running on the Dahme again. Swerving to miss an oncoming bus so that they have to drive through a puddle, she shouts for joy, taps Viktor, sitting up front, on the shoulder, and says, "Did you see that?" She eyes Thilde critically with a sidelong glance and shakes her head in irritation, as if not understanding how somebody could be so glum. Then she starts to sing. When she gets to the one about the changeable moon, she even remembers the lines she'd forgotten years ago: For earthly things bloom but a season, and wither away all too soon. Her most appreciative listener is the driver, who assures

151

her that if he could drive with no hands, he certainly wouldn't spare the applause. He later comes up with the expression "The older, the bolder!" which Tita acknowledges by laughing proudly.

The village they're headed for is no bigger than Görtz, just more lively. Flocks of gray-faced old people trip through the streets, the sidewalks being too slick. The driver circles the church then asks for directions. They are told to take an unpaved road out of the village. What from a distance looks like woods turns out to be a graveyard. They drive for ages past untended graves until the road ends at a barrier. A man yells from the window of the gatehouse that visiting hours are Sunday. Viktor gets out and shows the referral slip. Now they're allowed to pass, and they enter a city of barracks.

The sun has lured many of the elderly outside. They lean in open windows, sit in front of doors, shuffle around in slippers. The car glides at walking speed through rows of old people. The smell that fills the vehicle is atrocious. "It stinks here!" says Tita and turns up her nose.

The road gets better behind the closely built barracks, which seem to date from the war. The newly constructed administrative office is located between park grounds. "End of the line. Everybody out!" calls the driver, and Tita says cheerfully, "Well, then, no use acting tired now!" before struggling out of the vehicle.

While the driver is busy striking up a conversation with one of the men laying asphalt between the administrative office and the clinic, Tita, Thilde, and Viktor go inside. Tita, leading the way, courteously greets a man in a white coat, but he simply points her to the registration window and hurries past. Of the person sitting at the window, only the hands are visible: they take the slip, leaf through files, give out a number, and point to the right toward a counter where Tita's suitcase has to go. A woman checks to make sure it doesn't contain anything unnecessary. Thilde is given a nightshirt back. The suitcase is numbered with chalk. A man behind the counter grabs the suitcase, swings open the countertop, says "Please, say good-bye," and takes Tita by the arm. "Damn it, don't touch me, I don't even know you," Tita manages to say before a swinging door with frosted-glass windows slams shut behind her. The cigarette the driver lit upon arrival hasn't been finished by the time Thilde and Viktor exit the building.

The crowd between the barracks has grown. The car advances at a crawl, often having to stop because the old people are reluctant to move aside. Then they're surrounded by faces, faces hard to look at not because they're ugly or sickly, but because they're devoid of any expression at all, stolid and immobile; the eyes that follow the car mechanically are entirely blank.

Even after passing the gatehouse, the driver does not speed up. He drives past the fields of graves at a walking pace and stops when the village comes into view again. "If I were you," he says without turning around, "I'd order the driver back. 'Cause that old lady needs to be picked up again. Dying, I'd think, should at least be a little fun. And it's clear that that ain't possible back there. Think it over. You've got two minutes." He gets out and disappears behind the cemetery bushes. "Well?" he asks, back behind the wheel. He is wordlessly instructed by Viktor to keep on driving and refrains from any further remarks.

They get out in Arndtsdorf instead of being dropped off at New Glory. The lake, on which ice anglers stand unmovingly, is still covered with snow. Long shadows glide before Viktor and Thilde as they cross it. Sitting on a pier on the Prötz side, they wait for sunset before setting off into the woods, making a detour around May Valley. The mild west wind that was blowing in the daytime is warmer still in the evening, and the northern slopes have also begun to thaw. The woods come to life. Wet loads of snow come plopping to the ground. Disencumbered boughs spring up. Dead branches snap. Rain and snow fall from rustling treetops. Bedraggled, the two of them arrive at New Glory at dinner time. They slip into Thilde's room unseen and don't turn on the light. Only at midnight does their hunger drive them into the kitchen, where Olga, as though she knew the two of them would have a reason to celebrate, has abundantly laid the table for them.

Come morning, they decide not to start their quotidian existence just yet. At sunrise they leave the house (this time in rubber boots) and are greeted on marshy fields by the song of the lark. Ice floes drift on high water in the Hoppschugge, flowing brown and murky. The abandoned mill, not far from Frau Bahr's house, seems ghostly in its neglect. Thilde and Viktor pass through rooms bereft of windows and doors, convert them in their minds into living space, and inhabit them with kids and cats, until the card reader's Pomeranian drives them away with its furious yapping.

The first humans they encounter this day are two men in anoraks, pacing up and down outside of New Glory. Thilde and Viktor are greeted amicably as they run into them at the corner, on Dead Man's Road: "Good morning, Comrade Kösling! There's someone here who's waiting to see you."

GUEST OF HONOR

Viktor's father brings the rest home back to life. He's made the trip by sleigh, despite the thaw, a three-hour journey, mostly through woods, which the Haflingers managed with ease. He pulls into New Glory cracking his whip. Gabi and Thomas, whom he picked up in Görtz, are the first to jump off. The coachman, who sat by watching for hours because J.K. was driving, has little to do even now. He supervises as the children unharness the horses, inspects the empty cowshed, and looks on while the horses are fed. J.K. stretches his stiffened limbs, gives Olga, standing in the door of the house, a hearty handshake, and, motioning with his arm to include the coachman and children, says, "We're hungry as wolves."

He sets up headquarters, as he calls it, in the lounge, because that's where the television is, always on, mostly muted. It's impossible to tell if J.K. even sees what's being broadcast. Only once does he comment on the weather. He's worried about the trip back, but the coachman sets his mind to rest.

J.K. is not quite as big as Sebastian, but fatter. He likes to eat and eat a lot, and he makes no bones about it either. "You can see where it goes," he says, sticking out his gut, and enjoys being able to raise a laugh. Since no meal is good when you eat alone, he commands the children, the coachman, Sebastian, and Olga to join him, though not his other travel companions. He generously praises the farmer's breakfast he orders, with lots of bacon and onions, and insists that the others praise it too, in word and deed. "Eating is human, and the more you eat, the more human you are," he says, loading a second help-ing onto every plate without paying heed to protest. He is offended that Püppi, as usual, refuses to eat. "Impossible," he says, and sets the screaming child on his knee.

This is how Viktor finds his father: surrounded by people who chuckle at his attempts to teach a small child to eat and who learn in the process that it's no contradiction to be famous and powerful yet still enjoy life's simple pleasures. He finds him, then, as always—the educator—and, as always, feels embarrassed about it. Although ashamed of his father, he can't help feeling a certain admiration; while not wanting to be like him, he considers it his personal failing that he couldn't be if he tried. Unlike those who feel honored by the legend-ary Kösling's attempts to curry their favor, Kösling junior is repulsed by it. He sees through his father—but not entirely. He recognizes the changing masks for what they are but doesn't know what's behind them, apart from an unnerving vitality.

It is evident even in his struggle with the child that Kösling's lust for life triumphs over Püppi's defiance. With tears in her eyes, the child not only bravely swallows the bacon but asks for more amid resound-ing cheers.

Only now is it time to greet his son. It's a hail-fellow-well-met kind of greeting, but not without sincerity, with a slap on the back and a handshake, but no hug. The son, who's anywhere but where he should be, that is to say, at his desk, is called a son of a gun, whereas the father refers to himself as the old man. He popped over from the hospital to check up on him. He doesn't have a lot of time, doctor's orders for one thing, for another because of this blasted thaw. A sleigh, after all, is not a boat.

Olga takes the hint. She clears the table and shoos the children away—with force in Püppi's case, having attached herself to J.K.'s pant leg. Leaving the room, Olga gives Viktor a nod of pity. She seems to have an inkling of what he's got coming.

Viktor is uneasy, but not fearful. Even without thinking things through in advance, he feels he is well prepared, because he knows that the vigor about to assail him will be rendered ineffective: he'll let it run dry by being passive. It's the way he's reacted ever since childhood, the way he's avoided explosions and learned to put up with the undisguised contempt J.K. shows him, however unjust he finds it, because what the father dislikes about his son is the very thing he demands of him: his being the eternal pupil. Now, surprisingly, the pedagogue does not play his part. He demands not submission but compassion from his son, so that Viktor suddenly feels at sea. He doesn't know how to react to a father who finds the role of the strong man, the part he was just playing, ridiculous, who refers to himself as a wreck of a man, ready for the scrap heap, and who uses words like misery, despair, and grief. Viktor can neither feel nor show the sympathy expected of him. All he can do is wait and see whether or not he finds out what purpose the new mask serves, if it is a mask at all.

The wait is a long one, because the metaphorical noose J.K. uses to describe his sense of suffocation is made up of multiple strands. The main thread, around which the others are wound, is his prostate gland or, rather, its infirmity, prostatitis—a name J.K. is incapable of uttering without scorn in his voice. He calls it an old man's disease, the stupid inflammation of some silly gland around the urethra that swells up and squeezes it so that the contents of his bladder can escape only a drop at a time. As if the painful burning sensation weren't bad enough, the laughter of his comrades, veiled behind expressions of sympathy, only makes things worse. Because you can't very well hide an illness that forces you to get up and leave ten times during a three-hour meeting. J.K. knows what they're thinking: that the lover of wine, women, and song is now only allowed to sing! And then the demeaning procedures at the doctor's office. Because the sickly gland—to hell with it if only you didn't need it!—happens to be located right next to your rectum, so that the doctor, fingers protected by rubber gloves, has to use the rear entrance to get to it, pretending it weren't a humiliation for the famous Jan Kösling, who stands there bent over, pants around his ankles.

Every illness, if it's not fatal, says Viktor's father, goes away or at least gets better. What remains are the insights you gain while forced to rest, each one a strand in the noose around your neck. You notice you're getting older. Of course, you knew that already, but now the knowledge is tangible experience. It's a shock to see yourself standing naked on the hospital scale. You notice that you no longer dream certain dreams at night, that women treat you differently, that you tire more easily. The ambition to be better fades away and the time you have left loses the sense of endlessness it once had.

A beastly business is what J.K. calls the fabled act of "finding yourself"—because all you find out is that you're disposable. Two months you're gone from work and things are running as smooth as ever. Two weeks is all it takes and no one misses you anymore. It's only common decency that keeps them from forgetting you altogether. The machinery you thought you controlled suddenly has no need for you. The boss turns out to be a figurehead; he doesn't direct, he personifies a director. His function is representative, because that's all he's capable of anymore. When J.K. finally mentions that he had the chance to do some reading in the hospital and came to the realization that he no longer really understands the young people supposedly slated to carry on his work, Viktor can tell by the sound of his voice that the waiting period is nearly up. And sure enough, with the change of topic comes a shift in emotion; self-pity and lament give way to accusation. It's time to talk about historiography—the newest variety, which irritates J.K. What others tout as a differentiated approach he blames for causing confusion. That's right, J.K. is for good old black and white. It used to be that everyone knew what Prussia was about; now people have started writing dissertations again about—or, rather, people are *supposed* to be writing them but don't bother. "Correct me if I'm wrong."

Viktor, knowing he would only offend his father by telling him he's misinformed, hastens to admit the sad fact of the matter but instantly puts a positive spin on it: thanks to the natural disaster, his stay has brought him closer to the people; the contact has served him well, at least as a human being, and may have even heightened his consciousness; and while falling behind in his work may be a cause of concern for him, it certainly isn't painful; because theory is important, but practice even more so, meaning the gain in experience more than outweighs the loss in knowledge acquisition, so that leaving the rest home he'll ultimately feel enriched. "Maybe I've become more of an adult during my stay here," he says, as seriously and humbly as possible, divesting the sentence he wanted to say—*I'm no longer a child you can lead by the nose!*—of the slightest hint of rejecting authority. And apparently he succeeds. For J.K. remains calm, keeps his eyes glued to the picture tube, and says matter-of-factly, "And you want to get married, eh?"

Instead of answering, Viktor begins by admiring his father for being so well informed, but then in his confusion manages only to come up with a few unfinished sentences like "Well, you know what they say . . ." until his tongue eventually comes untied. The cares allegedly weighing on him, but in reality troubling J.K., he unburdens on his father's heart, forestalling the lecture he should have had coming and turning the pedagogue into his confidant. He thus eludes the peril of having to contradict him, which he knows J.K. can't stand. In this way the conflict between inclination and obligation is not played out between father and son, but in Viktor himself, who would certainly come to grief, we hear, if the problem did not have a solution—which, given the lack of an antagonistic contradiction, Viktor readily accepts.

One issue, that of love, needs no elaboration between men; the brief dialogue "You think she's the one?"—"Absolutely!" is entirely sufficient. The other issue requires Viktor to do some explaining, however, for one thing because it's the more complicated one, but also so that Viktor can probe the extent to which his father is willing to help. Not without enthusiasm does he describe the working-class girl who would be worthy of the Kösling name in every respect if it weren't for two minor flaws, which (as his mother rightly observed already) in and of themselves can hardly be deemed flaws but become so in connection with his career in the foreign diplomatic corps. Said flaws are, first of all, her lack of education, particularly in foreign languages and political matters, which, with the requisite willpower, could obviously be remedied, and, second, family ties, which, on closer examination, don't deserve the name but in light of the relevant regulations are very real indeed and pose an obstacle to marriage for a man of his profession.

The phrase "forbid marriage," which J.K. inserts correctively here, is nearly drowned out by the television, hitherto presenting its pictures mutely but now with its volume restored. While "The Latest from Around the World" is giving agronomists in Buckow their say, Viktor agrees with his father, being forced to raise the volume of his speaking voice in the process, which robs a good deal of the expressiveness from the anguish he's supposed to be showing. Rather than interrupting the industrious steel workers and the speaker engulfed by thunderous applause, he waits for the cultural part, which once again is muted. He doesn't get very far with his remarks about the spirit and letter of the law, however, because J.K. soon realizes what he's getting at and bluntly cuts him short. True, these security precautions are not intended for everyone; they only apply to the few, but when they apply it's without exception, no matter if your name is Krause, Kunz, or Kösling. Then again, if he loves girls with mothers in the West more than he loves his career, he can always give up the career; there's more than enough work in this country.

Since Viktor nods with understanding and looks troubled during the weather report—which has to be heard as well as seen, causing a lull in conversation—his father eventually calms down again. He adopts a tone he considers chummy, the same one he uses at meetings to win the trust of his listeners: a soft and rather subdued tone in which phrases like "I can tell you confidentially . . ." or "This one is strictly off the record!" are nothing if not persuasive. He also uses his method for slow thinkers, arguing in question-and-answer style; he repeats the key words before settling the issue once and for all with the folksy vulgarity that appeals to the young.

Thus, Viktor's father asks himself about the state of affairs, says they are grave but not beyond hope, and as a solution advises patience, patience, patience. Because what is it we're talking about here? The love of his life that one mistakenly believes will never come again, or simply a symptom of sexual withdrawal? Although it is fair to assume the latter—a sexual urgency that blurs all the senses but one, that cripples the brain, clouds one's powers of judgment, and puts goals in the center that belong on the periphery—it's not so easy to tell. Of course, a chambermaid can easily become a goddess of love for someone who's leading the life of a monk when she's the only girl far and wide, but it doesn't have to be that way, it's not inevitable. What's to be done? There's only one remedy his father knows—keep your cool, wait until you regain your powers of discernment, don't do anything you can't undo—in other words, gain time. Because only time will tell what Viktor wants to know. If he, J.K., were in Viktor's shoes, why, he would get out of here as fast as possible, far away, for a year or two, and let time be the judge. If his great love fades away with time, then it wasn't the real thing after all. But if it does survive, J.K. is willing to pick up their talk where they left off—on a more solid footing this time around. But, truth be told, he doesn't believe it. He's an old hand, he says, by way of conclusion, a man who is long on experience. He knows about life and love, and knows well enough that his own son will never find the love of his life either, but will just keep on looking, and that only one thing will be certain at the end of all his pains and troubles: that it was all for nothing. Because, though every woman might have her charms (and it's this uniqueness that makes them so appealing to men), these are ultimately immaterial and never long lasting. Then, with a grin, comes the vulgar figure of speech that reduces all things female to a single organ and succinctly sums up his point of view that women are all the same.

The smile Viktor resolved to put on to acknowledge his father's absurdities can soon be dropped. Their father-son talk is interrupted, because in comes Püppi with a piece of meat. She walks over to Kösling senior, climbs onto his knee, and wants to keep playing the game she calls "More! More!" She's brought along the requisite audience: Olga, who's come to say that the coachman is eager to get back, and Frau Erika, who spreads out her arms but holds back on the embrace. Her eyes are full of tears of joy at being reunited again. She invites everyone up to her room, where the scent of coffee fills the air, cookies are heaped on a crystal dish, and the music plays ever so softly.

Thilde serves the coffee. "Aha," is all Viktor's father says when he hears her name. He doesn't keep his eyes on her—which offends his son at first but finally encourages him to see her with the old man's eyes. He pulls it off surprisingly well.

J.K. spends all his charm on Frau Erika. He seizes on every hint of a memory she offers up and spins them into stories. He lets her talk too, laughs profusely at a humble but magnificent past he calls the Golden Fifties, alludes to incidents that only Frau Erika can understand and which they chuckle over in disbelief—then displays a look of concentrated earnestness when Sebastian, the killjoy, brings up the rest home: the awful condition the buildings are in, hardly a pleasure for staff and guests, and a cadre shortage that is simply unacceptable.

If Sebastian's integrity were not so impeccable, Viktor would assume his criticism was scripted to set the stage for a proper departure. Because the visitor couldn't have asked for a better one. He pushes aside his coffee cup (having had only milk, doctor's orders), says, "Well, let's have a look at it then!" and sets off, in the accompaniment of the others, on a tour of house and yard. He knits his brow and shakes his head, asks a question, jots something down. His exclamation "So much unused potential here!" sounds promising indeed.

The sleigh has been harnessed. J.K. shakes everyone's hand. Püppi is given a kiss, Viktor a hug. "We'll see what can be done," he says from his seat on the sleigh, and it's hard to tell just who he's talking to. Then the whip cracks. The horses shake their flaxen manes and begin to pull, while outside the gate the staff of New Glory stands waving good-bye to Kösling the Great.

Sunday Outing

The bright springlike morning is lacking only spring's green. Viktor is able to enjoy the journey without a thought of their destination. Thilde cannot—but has learned to hide her gloom so as not to ruin Viktor's mood.

They got up early, picked up the flower arrangement they'd ordered in advance at the market garden in Görtz, and are now cycling to the train station, pushed along by the wind at their backs, a big red sun hanging in the pale blue sky before them. The villages have not yet come to life. Smoke rises up, a dog barks, a flock of birds detaches itself from a tree with a swish. Viktor feels like whistling or singing, but doesn't bother; he's too busy showing Thilde everything that gives him pleasure. Even the train is cause for delight: it's so empty they can kiss without being seen.

A long time passes before he gives up trying to force his good mood on Thilde. Although he knows what's oppressing her (it's oppressing him too, the only difference being he's able to suppress it), he asks her what's wrong and listens patiently to her laments about Tita. They're nothing new to him; he hears them daily and knows there is little he needs to add. All he has to do is listen, and he's good at that.

How much he dreads their visit to Tita becomes clear to him only when the first elderly people shuffle toward them on their way to the barracks compound. The cemetery, which they have to cross on foot this time, seems endless to him. When they reach the barrier, he realizes he'll only be able to stomach the sickening surroundings if he puts his nerves on hold and makes himself unfeeling, if he refuses to acknowledge the wretchedness around him that gives the lie to his take on life. He's safe only by saying nothing, touching nothing, by trying not to breathe; seeing and hearing and smelling, he is forced to think of other things in order to shut himself off.

The initial information they're given turns out to be incorrect. Tita is not in ward 3, the new part of the complex with a bright, crowded corridor, music in the background, and doors wide open. She's apparently in the barracks section, in number 13. It's deathly silent there. The nurse has never heard Tita's name but has lists she can consult, and does, in fact, find a Lüderitz. She accompanies the two of them down a windowless corridor to the end of the building. Old women line the walls, sitting motionless and mute. Thilde looks at Viktor imploringly but Viktor dodges her gaze.

The defensive posture Viktor has taken stands the test at Tita's bedside. He sees her gray, sunken cheeks, her mouth now seemingly smaller, her chin longer, thinks that this is what death looks like but is ultimately left unmoved. Thilde tries in vain to wake the sleeping woman. Tita's eyelids quiver slightly, lift up, then droop again. So hard is Viktor's armored shell that not even Thilde's pain can touch him. His presence feels superfluous.

The smell of feces filling the air suddenly rouses him from his lethargy. He slowly rises to his feet, goes to the door but discovers it has no handle. The grated window can be opened though. The cold air, a relief to Viktor, startles one of the eight women in the room. She folds her hands like a child and begs him to close the window again. Her neighbor wakes up now, too, and weeps.

Viktor avoids the sight of moribund faces by staring fixedly at Thilde. She frantically appeals to Tita, takes her by the hands, strokes her forehead but barely gets her to lift her eyelids; lackluster, bleary, expressionless orbs are all that's visible behind them. The trip was pointless, Viktor tells himself, drawing deep breaths to fend off his nausea in the hope that visiting hours soon end.

The nurse delivers him from his misery. She puts the flowers they brought in a vase and tells Thilde that there's no point shouting: "You

164

should have called to say you were coming, we would have kept her off her medicine."

Viktor is now ashamed of Thilde, who is much too loud and angry when asking about the toxins they've pumped into her grandmother. The nurse, however, is not authorized to give out such information. She refers her to a young female doctor whose face is prematurely marked by the suffering around her. She endeavors at first to react kindly to Thilde's indignant questions, but her voice grows louder when it's her turn to speak. So it is, she says, Thilde's assumptions are correct: her grandmother's dementia, unfortunately incurable, is subdued with the use of drugs; her compulsion to flee is inhibited, her peace of mind and body is regulated by chemical means. There's no doubt about it, lethargy and a lack of movement are not good for old people. On the contrary. But prolonging their way to the grave would require more staff with proper training, five to twenty times as many. They would have to live with the elderly day and night, work and talk, play games and take walks with them. The staff they have now only manages the bare minimum: feeding the weak, keeping them clean, washing the dead. This is work that money can't buy, pots of gold would not be compensation enough for being so close to misery, death, and decay. Anyone who thinks he's entitled to complain should ask himself first if he's able and willing to help. "If you promised me," she snidely remarks, "to come here for two hours a day and take your grandmother out for a walk, I'd promise you to take her off the medication." But she doesn't bother asking if Thilde or Viktor would even consider because she knows the answer already. People who don't have time for their next of kin, she adds heatedly, should think twice before pointing their fingers at others. They should just be honest about it and admit that a sick old woman has no place in our world of utility. As long as she can keep house and take care of the children, she's indispensable, but when she's in need of care herself, they ship her off to a home—in other words, they condemn her. Her crime is the inability to work; her punishment, exile and dispossession. She has to leave her lifelong home, the house she knows, to move in with strangers in a strange place, where she also learns what it's like to be deprived of love. At first they visit her once a month, then two or three times a year, then they stop coming altogether: her industrious children forget about her. The news of her death is nothing but a nuisance because her relatives have long since given her up for dead. "When I see how, day by day, the sorrow and fear in their faces grow," the doctor says, "drugs to help them forget seem the best way to ease their suffering."

Only when the barracks and gravestones are out of sight does Viktor awake from the state of numbness he's induced himself into. He's happy knowing that the horror is safely behind him, feeling the warm rays of the sun in his face and holding the hand of the girl he loves. He'd like to say that he'd never known how much life could be worth living, but he keeps it to himself because Thilde is silent and he doesn't dare wrench her out of her sadness. Even on the train, when he can stand her silence no longer, he betrays nothing of his good humor. He refutes the doctor, accusing her of being hostile to progress and achievement, explains that everyone, Thilde included, has a right to live his own life, then asserts that Tita is no longer conscious of the state she's in. But none of this comforts Thilde. She looks at him as though she were still seeing Tita's deathly countenance, hugs him now and then, but still remains mute.

The trip back to New Glory is beautified by a sunset. Viktor sees the last of it (bloodred flecks behind black pine trunks) from the window of his room.

Night is drawing near from the woods and the first stars are visible in the not yet darkened sky when a knock comes at the door like the blow of a hammer. It's Sebastian, the jealous watchman, but this time he doesn't want to duel. He just wants to pass on a message that came his way this morning by phone, a telegram he jotted down and now hands over with a gleeful expression. He waits for Viktor to read it, wishes him a pleasant trip, bows and doffs the hat he's not wearing, and expresses his hope of never having to see his next-door neighbor again.

The Pain of Departure

It would not be far-fetched to compare Viktor's condition this evening with an injury: at first, the shock of the blow prevents the pain
from being felt; the fact of being injured has to register first with your
consciousness before the nerve can signal pain; but then it comes full
force, the mind yields, and it fills the soul entirely; all feeling is reduced
to pain, reason goes silent, the organ of thought ceases to function,
consciousness perceives nothing but suffering, not even time, which
passes as usual, exercising its erosive effects; time washes away the
pain by degrees, undermines its power, helps you adapt to the situation, and gives room once more to reason so that thoughts—stanch
the bleeding, dress the wound, go to the doctor—become thinkable
in spite of the pain. To put it plainly: Viktor, rendered incapable of
thought and action by the telegram, abandons himself for an hour or
so to the pain of parting before eventually learning to ease the pain.

For example, by explaining to Thilde the manner of his suffering.
The theory of layers he develops in the process is naturally just an
imaginary construct, dividing the indivisible for the sake of explanation—that is to say, drawing boundaries where none exist. Thus, the
first layer of thought is that of pain, since we know that all beauty,
all value, nay, all meaning in life vanishes when, as of tomorrow, we
can no longer see, hear, and feel the one we love. This, the level of
consciousness, though cruel enough, is ultimately bearable, as it's able
to be interrupted—by external stimuli, forcing you to think of other
things, as well as by sleep—unlike the second layer, the substratum of

the soul, which disseminates permanent darkness and, whenever the consciousness forgets its suffering for a brief spell, blackens the bright spot then and there, the suddenness of which gives rises to the third layer: the aggressive spillover into the physical, the bodily pain that's impossible to localize. Is it the heart that throbs and convulses, the head, the stomach, the blood that freezes? We don't really know, but we sense it might do us good to be active.

And Viktor does just that—not, of course, by disputing the decision (made he knows where) and suffering what is for him the unusual agony of choice. Rather, as someone who's learned to be moved by others even when wanting to be a mover, he shifts his activity to the organizational sphere: he arranges his departure, packs his bags and boxes, before taking the edge off his pain by wallowing in it once more.

The new pain that hits him is Thilde's fault. Instead of trying to comfort him, she shuts herself off from him altogether. A telegram has ordered him to end his working vacation, to be in Berlin by Monday morning, and soon thereafter to fly abroad. Thilde reacts with a look of fright, and in response to his question of what he should do, says, "You've known the answer long enough," before lapsing into silence and bursting into tears. She cries and cries, does not deign to look at or speak to him, and thereby spoils the beauty his departure might have had. She accuses not with words but tears. That he's already asked Helgalein to give him a lift to the capital is to her apparently a form of treachery. Her face, increasingly marred by tears, sobs, and nose blowing, he hides on his breast to keep from seeing it. He strokes her hair and speaks with his eyes closed in a quiet, singsong voice. He repeatedly offers her his assurance that he loves her, says it's not farewell forever, he'll come back before his trip, he might not even make the trip at all. He promises to write every day, not to forget her for a minute, to send for her before long. He does all the talking in the half hour they have left together. All she can do is cry.

The distance between them grows, because Viktor is unable to cry himself. Her tears, he assumes, are to prove she's suffering more than him. She disfigures herself to punish him. By crying she lays the blame on him. She refuses words of clarification in order to torture him but only achieves the opposite: he shuns her pain, having enough of his own already, and withdraws his affection from the tear-stained girl.

After an exhausting experience like this, it's refreshing to spend a few minutes in Frau Erika's room, where everything is just like always. Coffee is sipped, the candy dish passed in his direction, the electric fire flickers, and the record player hums softly in the background. Frau Erika, having spent the first day of spring from head to toe in sky blue, also feels the pangs of departure but doesn't bother a soul, neither herself nor the prince. For she knows all too well that every departure is also an arrival, every end is a new beginning, even death is nothing but transformation. And when, she asks, is there a better time to leave and arrive simultaneously than in springtime, when the new rhythm of the sun imbues and rejuvenates all living things, and human beings can renew themselves as well, cell for cell? They just have to open up to its wonder-working rays, open up completely. And to demonstrate how human beings have to let in nature, she leans back, relaxed, in her easy chair, closes her eyes, and breathes out loud: deep and even breaths, very deep, with mouth agape.

She knows and understands that the prince's heart is hurting. And she has a remedy for it too, just a word, but one that can have a magic effect if you say it and think it often enough. It's the little word *enough*. You just have to understand it properly, in its progressive sense, that is—moving upward and forward—and not as poisonous resignation. It's the enough of the discoverer who leaves the island he's explored already in order to seek out ones unknown; the enough of the artist who, dissatisfied with his work, gives it up to the world after all, because he's driven to create a new and better one, hoping to attain the bliss of perfection—in vain, of course, as Frau Erika knows.

Helgalein wants to change her clothes for the trip back, so Viktor has to stand at the window. In the window's reflection he sees Frau Erika step up behind him, ever so close but without making contact. Her mouth is close to his ear as she offers him some words of wisdom for the road, which he only vaguely understands. She talks about the rungs of a ladder he should toil up then leave behind without wistful longing, about a vulgar here and now, a more pure and rarefied tomorrow, and also about a higher sphere where not having but being is the order of the day, where the will wills nothing but wanting, and where the realization grows that not perfection but the thirst for it brings happiness.

Helgalein is raring to go. Suitcases and boxes are already stowed in the car. With an emphatic gesture, Frau Erika extends her hand to her prince for a kiss—an act the prince, a docile pupil, carries out symbolically. Olga, with a sleeping Püppi on her arm, Gabi, and Thomas have showed up in the yard to wave good-bye. "Manuela," explains Olga, "won't be coming. Her eyes are swollen from all the crying. She hasn't stopped since she heard you were leaving and is afraid to show herself."

Thilde's absence causes Viktor's pain to swell enormously. He rushes back into the house while the motor is running. Thilde's door is closed, but she opens straightaway when he knocks. They throw themselves into each other's arms, clinging to each other in a passionate embrace. And so they stand for some little time, until Gabi comes and calls for Viktor.

Only when Helgalein wordlessly hands him a tissue does Viktor notice the residue of Thilde's tears on his neck and cheek. He commends how quickly she takes the curves on a muddy Dead Man's Road, but Helgalein fends off his praise: she's been driving this road for a decade now.

OFFICIAL BUSINESS

Olga's interlocutor is sitting at a desk with nothing on it but his folded hands; the man has virtually no hair on his head and two flecks of encrusted blood on his chin. Olga's gaze, against her will, keeps honing in on these remnants of his morning shave; his gaze is directed right past her, at the wall on which the room's sole ornament hangs: a portrait of the head of state.

The man behind the desk is the head of the local government, Müller by name. A bricklayer's apprentice during his youth, he went on to work as a cattle buyer, co-op chairman, and shop manager, until the office of mayor, which no one else wanted to fill, seemed a more desirable position. It was a mistake that gave him stomach ulcers, whose constant pain is a source of ill humor. He vents his spleen on others, who become ill-humored in turn. His condition is thus reinforced by its symptoms. A change of profession might restore Herr Müller's health, but without a replacement he is barred from doing so. In his dreams, he sees himself as an invalid pensioner. Granting police powers to the office of mayor would also redeem him. Vested with police authority, he would not have to justify the applications denied, and he wouldn't have to explain to the villagers the often bewildering regulations from his superiors at the district level.

The presumptuousness of his clients—always demanding explanations—he's learned to counter with monosyllabic replies. Whereas at home he makes do with varied grunts, at work he goes to the trouble of forming actual words, which he then can use as set formulas, although often at the expense of logic. Thus, for instance, when Olga explains that she has come to register the burial of Frau Lüderitz, he answers with a simple "No!" Condensing his reply as such, he manages to capture negation of every sort. And he doesn't hesitate to say it again when Olga, thinking she's been misunderstood, repeats her request. Only after the third "No" does she ask, "How come?" which elicits a fourth "No," along with a flourish.

The mayoral hands detach themselves from the desktop as well as from each other, open a drawer, take out a document, and slide it in Olga's direction. Instead of having it spoken out loud, she can read the answer to her question. It concerns resolution 79 slash 13 of the Görtz Town Council in which, under item 3, where Herr Müller's finger rests, it is clearly stated that only those who are registered with the police in the townships of Görtz or Prötz have a right to a plot in the local cemetery. This doesn't apply in Tita's case, Olga is quick to realize, because having moved into the nursing home, she was registered under a different address.

The mayor's view that the hearing is over isn't shared by Olga. He puts the document back in its place, takes a file off the shelf, and begins leafing through it while Olga lights up a cigarette (as a sign of her composure) and with the sentence "You've got to be kidding me!" launches into a long and unprepared speech dealing with the right to one's native soil even after death, in which the mayor's diapers are mentioned (because that's what he was still wearing when the deceased had the name of her husband chiseled onto a gravestone) as well as the long arm of the Ministry, which, Olga assumes, well exceeds that of a local head of government.

Her sermon has no noticeable effect. Even when she mentions the name Kösling, Müller remains mute. Only Olga's eyes, which keep getting stuck on the flecks of blood, have an unsettling effect on him. He grabs his chin, senses an uneven spot, rubs at it, ripping open the wound in the process, and adorns his handkerchief with dabs of red. Perhaps Olga has this harmless injury in mind when, back in the kitchen of New Glory, she calls the mayor not only a bureaucrat and brute, an ogre and fiend, but also a bloodhound, before offering Sebastian a piece of advice for the trip back to the mayor's office he plans to make accompanied by Thilde: "Kill the bastard!"

The opportunity does not arise, however. Of the many methods to avoid unpleasant encounters, Herr Müller has chosen the surest: not being there. Frau Fiedler, his secretary, suspects he's at home. At home, they fancy he's in the office. The salesgirl at the food co-op, with whom he often sits drinking milk, sends them to the constable, who thinks he's seen him at the calf shed. At the calf shed, they know for certain he's in his office. And since everyone they meet along the way offers their condolences and sings their praises of Tita, before they know it it's lunchtime. Frau Fiedler, a part-timer, calls it a day. She's positive now that Müller is in the district town; his automobile parked in front of the building is no reason to believe otherwise: what with gas being scarce, he could have hitched a ride with somebody.

"Just a minute," Sebastian says to the secretary, who has already slipped on her coat and is jangling her keys. He takes a seat in the mayor's chair, leisurely leafs through the telephone directory, and dials the desired office. "Görtz Town Council here," he says, his eyes trained on Frau Fiedler. "It concerns the late Frau Lüderitz. When, if I might ask, are you going to bring the coffin? The cemetery isn't easy to find. We need to know exactly when you're coming, so someone from the family can be there to meet the car at the entrance to the village."

He replaces the receiver, asks if Frau Fiedler has the key to the mortuary, and, as she mutely shakes her head, says never mind, he's got enough tools to open doors.

MAY VALLEY

Everyone's mind is on Viktor on the morning of the funeral, but no one talks about him as long as Thilde is seated at the table. She wired him the news of Tita's death. And even though he didn't answer, everyone is still expecting him.

It is thanks to Olga that breakfast isn't eaten in silence. The story she tells at the table, about the mayor of Görtz rejecting a corpse, is familiar to everyone except for one. And yet everyone is interested in the way she tells it, because she turns it into her own story by always inserting a generalizing "we" whenever the name Sebastian is due. "A call from us was all it took to make justice out of the law," she says. "And when at midnight the casket was where it belonged, the scoundrel didn't dare speak up. Not a word, not a peep came out of his mouth. He didn't even ask for repair costs."

The man at the table who is not yet familiar with the story of the triumph of human decency over bureaucratic obstinacy, and for whose sake it's being recounted, is a gray-haired bespectacled fellow by the name of Horst. As the new boss around here, he's allowed to sit where Max once did: at the head of the table. That Horst is from Lusatia is evident when he speaks—a seldom occurrence. He's sparing with words, sparing with gestures, and no one has yet to hear him laugh. Sebastian claims that his presence makes him yawn relentlessly. Olga, though, whose tolerance for male idiosyncrasies knows no bounds, appreciatively refers to him as a fine specimen of a man and can't understand the rumors, there before Horst was, that his wife just up and left him. She sets great store in him. Anyone filling this post just when the modernization of the rest home is getting under way, set in motion by Kösling the Great, will, she assumes, also be able to chuck his weight around and spare her from being transferred to the Oderbruch marshes. All she has to do is show him that she's got what he's surely lacking: self-assertiveness.

This is why she alone defeats the mayor. And why her tone is acerbic when she packs the children off to school, throws construction workers out of the kitchen, or prevents Püppi from climbing onto Horst's lap. Even Frau Erika, whom neither construction noise nor dirt could drive away from New Glory, gets a taste of Olga's resoluteness. When, dressed in black as befits the occasion, she interrupts the breakfast party to explain the reasons prohibiting her from attending the funeral ceremonies, Olga brusquely interrupts and sends her packing, remarking that it's up to her to know what she owes the dead.

Only when Horst leaves the kitchen, as silently as he came, does Olga's voice return to normal. She has questions of attire to sort through with Thilde and organizational matters to discuss with Sebastian; she has to knock at Frau Erika's door to let her know that she should send Viktor to the cemetery, for poor Thilde's sake, if he happens to show up; she has to take care of the funeral food; she has to change her clothes. No sooner has she attended to all of these chores than the pastor arrives.

The construction workers make noise with their tools as well as their radio. In the new window openings knocked into the wall of the cowshed, which is slated for conversion into sleeping quarters, they've set up a loudspeaker emitting the sounds of distorted music. It echoes in the yard amid mounds of mortar, rubble, and hodmen, accompanies the mourners down Dead Man's Road, and is even audible as a faint rhythmic hammering under the cemetery trees.

There are four of them in all—two couples, the way Olga sees it. Thilde next to the pastor up front, behind them Sebastian and herself. The pastor, a half-bald man who, arriving at New Glory, did not at all fit Olga's picture of a clergyman, has since slipped on his cassock and now (despite the prayer book wedged under his arm while walking) looks dignified. The other three are carrying daffodil bouquets, which is all the market garden in Görtz had to offer. Thilde has to fill the pastor in on the details of Tita's life. He's intrigued when, asked what her grandmother especially loved, Thilde brings up the song about the changeable moon. She complies with his request to sing it for him but doesn't get very far; she has to look for a handkerchief. Trying to take her mind off things, he tells her a little about himself: he's a lover of old songs and a collector of forgotten ones, even ones like this, which aren't really all that old. It reminds him of the more famous one: "We sit here together so gaily, and love one another so much." That's genuine Biedermeier, an era, he finds, that kind of resembles our own.

Olga is not particularly interested in what he means by "kind of," which the pastor subsequently endeavors to explain. She can listen with only half an ear anyway, because Sebastian, too, is talking nonstop. The Back Bush, his future park, which the workers have degraded to a gravel-storage area, is his preferred topic. It gives him frequent opportunity to discreetly turn himself around and keep an eye on New Glory, especially when he hears an automobile. But it's only ever construction vehicles hauling building materials, or small cars conveying mourners from Görtz.

Only when they reach the edge of the woods and climb the ever steeper path does a large automobile roll up with a single occupant. Even Thilde, having resisted the urge to look back until now, finally gives in, stops in her tracks like Sebastian and Olga, and lets the pastor, discoursing on the placid surface and seething underground of a far-off age, continue on his own. On the narrow hillside path, divided in irregular intervals by stairs, the three of them stand single file, awaiting Viktor: Sebastian in a black suit that seems to date from his confirmation; Olga, in her black stockings and black hat and a much too warm gray winter coat; and Thilde in a long, black silk dress that doesn't fit despite last-minute alterations (she looks like a child playing grandma).

But out of the vehicle alights a woman. From far away she looks young, but the impression wears off the closer she gets. Olga and Sebastian don't know her and, finding it unseemly to stare, they continue climbing the path, but come to a halt again when Thilde doesn't follow them. The woman sets the wreath she's been carrying up against a tree, arranges her freshly coifed hair with a self-conscious gesture, goes up to Thilde, who is coming to meet her, and embraces her. "My child," she says, so loud that even the pastor, standing above them among the graves, can hear it.

Thus, at the funeral service in the chapel he addresses not only the granddaughter but also the daughter of the deceased—causing a stir in the crowd of mourners, since everyone coming from Görtz, Prötz, Schwedenow, and Liepros wants to catch a glimpse of the long-lost woman. His portrayal of the difficult but rewarding life of the dearly departed becomes muddled as a result, and since the commotion fails to subside, he shortens his oration and lets the people sing instead.

Up on the hill at the open grave, in front of the memorial stone already bearing the dead woman's name, he has problems making himself be heard. It's not the wind, blowing in gusts and causing his cassock to flutter, that is so disturbing, but the chugging sound of dump trucks unloading their trash nearby. Although the pastor, having conducted enough burial services here before, has learned to let his gaze wander beyond the landfill to the treetops and distant fields, he's powerless against the noise. His prayers are lost in the clamor of engines, and no matter how loud he intones "Jesus Christ, my sure defense," it's no match for the clatter caused by thousands of empty tin cans tumbling down the slope.

In a cloud of ash garnished with paper scraps, Thilde and her mother receive condolences. Well disciplined, each of the mourners queues up in an orderly fashion in the line of sympathy-wishers, does his duty, then rushes back to the protective hillside. The pallbearers, Griepenkerl included, finish their burial work, and apart from Thilde only Sebastian is left. The latter has gained a new insight that he's itching to get off his chest: the tears you shed at the graveside, he proclaims, wiping his own from his beard, are not for the dead person at all. They're for yourself, having been reminded of your own mortality. Thilde covers the burial mound with daffodils and arranges the wreaths so that the inscriptions on the ribbons are legible. The prettiest wreath was contributed by the "grateful daughter," the biggest one by Frau Erika Schulze-Decker, with a motto for the deceased to take along with her on her journey: Love never faileth!

She says something similar to Thilde shortly afterward. Having pushed her way toward her in the lounge, where Olga has loaded up the enormous dining table with cake and canapés, she's now sitting (in a black dress with white lace trim) between Thilde and the pastor (who once again looks like Joe Blow), shows her the telegram in which Viktor regrets being only able to attend in spirit, and lifts her up emotionally. Whether or not love lives or dies, she says, trying to look deep into Thilde's eyes, can only be decided by the one who loves; for love is not a gift, but the result of your inner, spiritual work and, as such, is not subject to external influences; it is capable, provided pessimism and resignation don't debilitate it, of transforming reality according to its needs and desires; because man, the master of nature, has a chunk of nature in himself.

The plaudits she earns come not from Thilde, who stares at the telegram without even listening; it is roly-poly Frau Bahr from the wilds of Hoppschugge, who, mouth stuffed with streusel cake, nods her approval at every word. She cries out, "Yep, that's exactly what *she* always says; you can't give up hope, you've got to hold on to it, always; because once you lose hope, there's nothing left."

RECOVERY

Exhausted from the strain of saying good-bye, Viktor closes his eyes
for a few minutes on the airplane. He'd like to sink into obliviousness
and let his fear of flying wear off, but having tuned out the buzz of
conversation around him, he ends up instead in a state of concentration in which he thinks of nothing but himself. He's waiting for the
pain, which should be settling back in right now, but senses nothing of
it. All that's there is a murmur, caused by the void and not unpleasant.
He feels a lightness akin to well-being, if not for the lack of cheerfulness, a comfort that's nothing but the absence of suffering. The term
convalescent comes to his mind: though weakened still by illness, he is
on the road to normality.

The command to fasten seat belts tears Viktor out of his inward
absorption. As always, fear sets in when the plane begins to taxi but
goes away after takeoff. He sees woods, fields, roads, and lakes pass by
below and without realizing at first what it has to do with his condition, he thinks of Frau Bahr, who, Thilde says, runs into the meadow
to wave whenever an airplane flies over her lonely house. She likes to
think that her husband, a *Luftwaffe* pilot missing in action since the
war, is still alive, that he hasn't come home yet for mysterious reasons
but often flies over to give her a sign. It is she who comes to Viktor's
mind—because he's been fortunate to escape a sickness which she
succumbed to irredeemably: the stability of feelings. He pictures
the disease in varied images: as a hardening of the heart; as a tumor,

unceasingly producing a noxious, pain-inducing bile; as a stone in the soul, impossible to purge.

The convalescent leans back in his upholstered seat. His eyes meet those of a stewardess, whose professional smile becomes a personal one when Viktor smiles back at her. The joy he feels reminds him of one he has felt in the past, and it's not hard for him, once the girl disappears to the front of the plane, to picture in place of her pale complexion a swarthy one instead. This causes the pain to resurface, the pain he thought he had left behind, or traces of it anyway, enough at least to unburden his conscience once he's worked it out. The letter he writes upon reaching normal altitude will contain a detailed account of it.

AFTERWORD

When the German Democratic Republic, or GDR, imploded in the fall of 1989, Günter de Bruyn was ranked among its top men of letters. In the turbulent years that followed, at a time when East German literature was rapidly losing currency, indeed its very legitimacy being called into question by the so-called *Literaturstreit* or "literary debate," and when other leading East German writers were attacked in a media-fueled witch hunt for their collaboration with the SED regime, de Bruyn succeeded in consolidating his reputation as an all-German writer. He was touted by critics as a model of artistic integrity, particularly after the publication of his two-volume memoir. Now in his eighties, he has since gone on to become a prolific essayist and cultural historian. He is the author of more than thirty works of fiction and nonfiction and has received more than a dozen prestigious literary awards in the last two decades alone. While he ceased writing fiction in reunified Germany, de Bruyn the fiction writer has remained a household name to many East Germans, a name that elicits smiles of recognition for the ironic novels and stories he wrote more than twenty-five years ago, most of which are still in print. And yet little is known of him outside Germany. This translation, his first major work to be published in the United States, hopes to redress this neglect.

Günter de Bruyn was born on November 1, 1926, in Berlin to a Bavarian Catholic father (with Dutch ancestors) and a Prussian Protestant mother. His early years were typical of his generation: Hitler Youth (mostly truant), paramilitary training, conscription as an antiaircraft auxiliary, or "ack-ack gunner," as a teenager, and frontline duty at the end of the war. His brief stint as an inept and unwilling eighteen-year-old soldier ended on Easter Sunday 1945 with a shrapnel wound to his skull during an engagement with the advancing Red Army. The aphasia he suffered as a result of his injury robbed him of his powers of speech. Yet not being able to speak when the unspeakable was happening around him was, in hindsight, a blessing in disguise. He would slowly relearn his language while postwar Germany picked up the pieces.

Released from a military hospital in Western Bohemia at the end of the war, he returned to Berlin by foot, where he was eventually reunited with his mother. De Bruyn briefly worked as a teacher in the countryside, then from 1949 to 1953 studied library science in East Berlin. In 1953, the same year a workers' uprising was quelled with Russian tanks in cities throughout East Germany, he accepted a position at the Central Institute for Library Studies in East Berlin, a job he held until 1961, the year the Berlin Wall was erected. It was then that he devoted himself fully to writing.

His first novel, *The Ravine* (1963), was a largely autobiographical and, by his own admission, overly ideological account of his wartime experiences. Awarded the prestigious Heinrich Mann Prize from the Academy of Arts the following year, he later disowned the work for the compromises he made to ensure its publication (but held on to the prize money, a sizable sum). His literary breakthrough came in 1968 with the novel *Buridan's Ass*, a social satire and modern-day tale of adultery set in mid-1960s Berlin which marked his coming of age as a writer and also brought him to the attention of Western readers and critics. The novel's ironic undertone and the penetrating psychological portrait of its protagonist (a librarian who leaves his wife for a younger intern but fails to make a new start in life and live up to his youthful ideals) would be characteristic of his works to follow. Two subsequent short novels, *Prize-Giving Ceremony* (1972) and *Investigations in the Mark Brandenburg* (1978), deal with opportunism and careerism in the academic world. The latter concerns the conflict between a successful historian in East Berlin and his unexpected rival in the form of a provincial schoolteacher and hobby historian—

both of whom have spent years researching the same dead poet, with radically different conclusions. The works solidified his reputation as a keen observer of the foibles and moral conflicts of East German intellectuals.

His fifth and final novel to date, *New Glory*, was published in 1984, first in West Germany and a year later in the East. Despite the work's "ideological weaknesses," pointed out in a reader's report, the manuscript was approved for publication in East Germany in 1983, having cleared both in-house censors and official censors at the Ministry of Culture with only minor changes being "negotiated" with the author. (The sentence "Pills make life shorter," for instance, was expunged from the nursing home chapter—Communists, mind you, are life-affirming—and Viktor's father, originally portrayed as a member of the Central Committee, was taken down a notch.) While the book's publication was delayed due to production bottlenecks, a licensed edition under way in the West was ultimately published first and would unwittingly seal its fate in the East, at least for the time being. Western critics were quick to pounce on the book's negative critique of GDR society—"Viktor to marry beneath his station. The most radical novel to date by East Berliner G. de Bruyn," etc.—causing East German authorities to reconsider their decision. De Bruyn's publisher felt compelled to issue a self-critical declaration: "The potential of exploiting de Bruyn's novel for communist-baiting, though taken into consideration by the publisher when approving the manuscript, was altogether underestimated compared to what we're seeing now." De Bruyn was expected to follow suit and publicly declare the Western reviews to be "grave distortions." When he refused to do so, the manuscript was sent back to the ministry, where, after nervous deliberation weighing the dangers of "long-term damage" at home and abroad, its authorization was revoked. Twenty thousand printed copies, none of which had made it to East German bookstores, were pulped. The author's contract with his publisher was cancelled. (The author's fee, however, as if to punctuate the capriciousness of publishing practices in the GDR, was paid out in full.)

De Bruyn had long been uncomfortable in his role as an East German writer, as the cultural representative of a state which in his eyes had no legitimate claim to existence. In his second volume of memoirs, *Forty Years*, he described this ambivalent position as follows:

> I was indebted to both sides, existentially to the East, on whose territory I lived, earned my money and had established a reputation, intellectually and morally to the West, where I felt at home with my views and interests. . . . [I] vacillated between visions of heroic cries of protest and waking nightmares ending in publication bans and prison sentences. I blamed myself for having missed the opportunity to flee, dreamed of writing censor-free in West Berlin or Hamburg, and at the same time found it absurd to leave the region I belonged in without an immediate threat to my life. I was proud of sticking it out despite the oppression, but despised myself for settling down, afraid that sooner or later I would wind up a provincial idiot.

Like many writers in the GDR, de Bruyn was permanently subject to the efforts of a rapacious state to co-opt him as an artist (not least of all its failed attempts to recruit him as a Stasi informer) and viewed every success as a potential act of collusion. Indeed, cultural ideologues in the East would hold up his work as proof of their tolerance and cultural diversity—while tapping his phone and placing him under surveillance (his secret police file dates back to 1964). So the book's being banned was something of a personal watershed, a chance to set the record straight. "I was off the beaten track now, the place where I belonged," he reflected in retrospect. "My strained relations with the state were finally out in the open."

Predictably, banning the book only heightened awareness of it and attracted even more reviews in the Western press. Copies of the Western edition were meanwhile being smuggled eastward, and respected colleagues of de Bruyn came to the writer's defense until cumulative pressure both internal and external finally convinced East German authorities to reissue authorization. A drastic about-face and face-saving gesture, the move was smugly described in Stasi files as an ideological victory over "enemy attempts to play up de Bruyn as an 'opposition writer' and exploit him in a smear campaign against the cultural policy of the GDR" while "helping to break down [de Bruyn's] confrontational attitude and strengthen the effects of social disciplining," a statement unmistakably reflecting the state's view of itself as a disciplinarian, trying to keep its artists in tutelage. (Deputy Cultural Minister and "head censor" Klaus Höpcke actually summoned de Bruyn to his office to inform him in person that the novel would be published. When de Bruyn asked why, Höpcke responded, "It's better we didn't ask. Let's just be happy about it.") The East German edition hit the shelves in 1985.

The novel is typical of de Bruyn's oeuvre and of his development as a writer. *New Glory* tells the story of Viktor Kösling, the not-so-talented son of a high-placed functionary. Before entering the diplomatic service of his country and rising to the ranks of its political elite, Viktor heads to a secluded, state-run vacation home by the name of "New Glory" to write his long-overdue dissertation, a prerequisite to his career advancement. Instead of working, he falls in love with the chambermaid, Thilde, a girl of simple means. His overbearing parents catch wind and intervene, especially upon discovering that the girl's mother lives in the capitalist West—a political liability to a socialist parvenu. Viktor eventually gives in to the pressure, leaving a trail of destruction behind him. What begins, then, as a lighthearted love story develops into dark tragicomedy.

On the surface the work is a realist novel—the late-nineteenth-century writer Theodor Fontane or the modernist Thomas Mann come to mind, both of whom greatly influenced de Bruyn. The novel, in fact, draws considerably on two works in particular: Fontane's *Irrungen, Wirrungen** with its jilted bride from a lower social station, and Mann's *The Magic Mountain* with countless parallels (and contrasts) in theme, plot, and character. To cite just a few examples: the remote, retreat-like settings, in Mann's a mountain sanatorium in the Alps, in de Bruyn's a vacation and rest home in the "flatlands" of East Germany; the protagonists' infatuation with quasi Oriental women, i.e.,

---

*Translated into English at least four times, with as many titles: *Trials and Tribulations* (1917), *A Suitable Match* (1968), *Entanglements* (1986), and *Delusions, Confusions* (1989).

185

Clavdia Chauchat with her Russian accent and "Kirghiz eyes" and Klothilde Lüderitz, the lisping chambermaid with skin redolent of India; a "magic-mad" Walpurgis Night and "hellish" party scene midway through; both men's "recovery" at the end of the novel after succumbing to illnesses more emotional than physiological, a recovered Hans Castorp being sent from the rarified heights of a Swiss sanatorium to his death (presumably) in the battlefields of the Great War, whereas a recovered Viktor Kösling takes an opposite trajectory, from the flatlands to the skies, in an airplane bearing him westward, toward his future career as a diplomat. These parallels are anything but derivative but consciously invite comparisons between the social mores of then and now, at least the now of East German readers.

Which brings us to an obvious but salient point: *New Glory* is a novel written in a specific cultural context, namely, the GDR. In an authoritarian state like the GDR, with social, economic, and cultural policies dictated from above, social criticism was often tantamount to a critique of power. Hence politics and literature were deeply intertwined. This political component of the book was obvious to most East German readers, less so perhaps to today's Western readers.

The inhabitants of New Glory are introduced as "one big family," and New Glory is indeed a kind of microcosm of society in late communist East Germany. Life here, it seems, is hardly idyllic. The very setting of the novel—a rundown farmstead in a remote corner of the Mark Brandenburg cut off from the rest of the world by a snowstorm—can be taken as an allegory of East Germany as a walled-in (snowed-in) state. Each character in the book tries to escape from an oppressive reality, each in his or her own way: Sebastian by getting back to nature; Frau Erika by living in a mythical, fairy-tale world; Olga through nicotine and alcohol; Tita by living in the irretrievable past. Sebastian, the gardener, disillusioned with climbing the ladder of success, drops out of society altogether and pursues his quasi-Thoreauvian ideal in the backwaters of New Glory, while Thilde, an unassuming chambermaid, dreams of a life in the lap of luxury— Viktor's world. Only Viktor, the fortunate son of a political functionary, has the means at his disposal to transcend oppressive borders, but tragically lacks the emotional maturity and willpower needed to become a self-determined individual. Alas, Viktor, the chameleon *par excellence*, is used to "being the person people want him to be."

In his volume of essays entitled *Writing in the Dark*, Israeli novelist David Grossman "addresses the conscience of a country that has lost faith in its leaders and ideals" (to quote the book's flap copy). Grossman writes:

> When a country or a society finds itself . . . in a prolonged state of incongruity between its founding values and its political circumstances, a rift can emerge between the society and its identity, between the society and its "inner voice." . . . A special kind of language then begins to emerge, one that is usually a manipulation on the part of those who wish to prolong the distorted situation. . . . It depicts a reality that does not exist, an imaginary state constructed by wishful thinking . . . . In such conditions one of our most dubious talents arises: the talent for passivity, for self-erasure, . . . the talent for being a victim.

The GDR, like all Soviet satellite states, was a political construct built on grandiose promises backed by Soviet might. In October 1961, the Twenty-second Party Congress of the CPSU outlined "The Bright Future of Mankind" in its new "Party Program on Achieving Communism." Khrushchev boldly proclaimed that by the year 1980 Communism would be firmly established throughout the Eastern bloc. The Soviet sphere was to have surpassed the West economically, work would be a source of fulfillment rather than compulsion, the distinction between town and countryside would disappear, and social divisions would be a thing of the past; food and housing would be available virtually for free, money and crime all but abolished; even the problem of aging would by then have been tackled by Soviet scientists. Or so the official Party organ in East Germany, *Neues Deutschland*, reported. Needless to say, things did not go according to Plan. By 1980, East Germans were not living in a communist paradise but in "really existing socialism," defined as an in-between stage of development on the path to mature communism—a radical revision of the revolutionary goals once proclaimed by communist leaders.

In this respect, even the novel's name is an implied criticism of official ideology. Although *Neue Herrlichkeit* (in German) does exist on the map, its choice as the novel's title clearly highlights the discrepancy between official propaganda and reality. Just as Viktor's dissertation is all talk and no substance, so GDR society with its aspirations as a progressive humanist state has failed to materialize. The New Man of socialist society is Viktor, with his "talent for passivity." Moreover, the central conflict between Viktor, a member of the new political elite, and Thilde, a working-class girl, shows how the supposedly classless society of East Germany, the so-called land of workers and peasants, is clearly marked by social divisions. These were not a "relic of the bourgeois past," as most contradictions with official ideology were euphemistically referred to, but stemmed from new power structures, where not money and property counted (as they do in the capitalist West), but political allegiance to the powers that be.

Frau Erika, the wife of an antifascist hero, probably best portrays the fantasylike character of official ideology. As a representative of the "old guard"—a nod to the GDR's founding myth as an antifascist state—Frau Erika enjoys the privileges of a new regime. (Her access to "good-quality coffee" is an obvious indication of the connections she enjoys which average East Germans did not.) Yet her belief in a better future, however genuine it may have been, has effectively degenerated into "wishful thinking." The ideals of a glorious communist future have been transformed into a diffuse belief in spiritual progress, in a "pure and rarefied tomorrow." The "vulgar here and now" is explained away by a theory of reincarnation; the liberation of mankind from its economic fetters has been replaced by the "emancipation of the soul." Frau Erika, we learn, had once been an actress, and she still hasn't cast off her single greatest role: the minister's wife. Standing on the dignitaries' platform in the capital on national holidays, she waves to the denizens of New Glory, who watch from home on their television sets. The reader is left wondering if it's all just an act or a symptom of self-delusion. (Her fairy-tale correspondence with Viktor would suggest the latter.)

Yet the novel is much more than mere satire and social commentary. It is a tribute to de Bruyn's art that his handling of the political is never programmatic, that he always maintains a sufficient ironic distance from his characters, and that his characters, while certainly representative of GDR society, are never stock figures, but living, breathing, aching individuals. *New Glory* is an eminently psychological novel, and it is this aspect that gives it its universal appeal (along with its humor). Two of the leading protagonists, Viktor and Sebastian, are also two of the book's most ambivalent (hence realistic) characters. Both are in their own way likable. Viktor for his open ear and willingness to please, his ineptitude and optimism, even his laziness. On the other hand, we see him as the spoiled child of influential parents who, outwardly polished and glib, can certainly be cynical when he wants to be. Sebastian, by contrast, is outwardly gruff and rough around the edges. We can't see through his bearded face. But we can feel for his decision to drop out of society and lead a self-determined lifestyle ("There's no work that compares to making plans of your own, and that's exactly what everyone's being denied these days"). His treatment of Thilde is crude and insensitive, yet only Sebastian has the courage to stand up to a hard-nosed local bureaucrat ("the triumph of human decency over bureaucratic obstinacy"), and only he seems to have a vision of truth and honesty we can relate to. Sebastian may be a curmudgeon and pessimist, but he hasn't been corrupted by the system. He still has his "inner voice" and isn't afraid to speak his mind.

New Glory is likewise a novel about love. About the mechanisms of deceit we perpetrate against ourselves and others (Viktor the "deceiver deceived" while his casual lover exults in her "newfound glory"). Viktor is a piece of every one of us when we turn the ones we need into the ones we love. Love, the ostensibly most selfless of virtues, devolves in the novel into a game of possession and control, a tendency strengthened by a deforming environment. Critic and translator Michael Hofmann writes (with reference to Wolfgang Koeppen and his trilogy of novels from the 1950s about the state of affairs in West Germany):

[H]ow . . . can there be anything as frail and contingent as human happiness, as long as the macro-scene is so full of iniquity? Surely everything . . . is warped, if not crushed, by the weight of these bigger tensions and untruths. Love is perhaps the most degraded thing of all: a feeling produced from cynicism, opportunism, or vacancy, a transaction somewhere on the scale between seduction and rape. In a world of rubble, where is one going to find a rose garden? . . . Tyranny has been described as the mother of metaphor, in which case, love—a state of emergency, a politics of two . . . perhaps might qualify as a form of tyranny.

And yet we are almost willing to believe Viktor's self-deception, unlike Viktor's openly cynical father, J.K.: "[W]hat is it we're talking about here? The love of [Viktor's] life that one mistakenly believes will never come again, or simply a symptom of sexual withdrawal . . . , a sexual urgency that blurs all the senses but one?" His sober arguments not only reflect his own personal emotional truth, distilled from bitter experience, but are politically expedient as well, as he uses them to pressure Viktor into giving up his fiancée. Paternalism, of course, is fatherly love. And what is it that communist leaders professed to have for their subjects if not the loving desire to perfect them, as in Orwell's "Ministry of Love," the secret police and torture chambers of Oceania, or Dostoyevsky's "Grand Inquisitor"? *New Glory*, though a novel of love, is once again a novel of politics. Love as the handmaiden of tyranny.

De Bruyn's novel can be placed in a period of stagnation and resignation, the late phase of East German history when many were content to settle into a comfort zone, their niche in society, and accept prevailing conditions. In *Forty Years*, de Bruyn described the situation as follows:

The masses had learned to content themselves with moderation, and the leaders, too, were coming to accept their populace. While still promulgating their inviolable doctrine, the sole foundation of their legitimacy, they largely abandoned their audacious political objectives. Order and prosperity had become the new watchwords, gradually supplanting progress and victory. Enthusiasm was only demanded of those who wanted to get ahead, subordination sufficed for the rest. The most effective agitprop slogans were comfort and security.

Tita embodies this sense of quiescence and resignation. Although her long life has taught her to be distrustful of governments run by men with facial hair, whether Kaiser Wilhelm, Hitler, or Party leader Walter Ulbricht with his goatee, she has also learned to accept the status quo. Her name has been marked on her gravestone for decades. Her pet phrases are "No use complaining!" and "What must be, must be." And her favorite game is "Aggravation," whose German name, it is worth pointing out, has a decidedly different twist: *Mensch ärgere dich nicht!* (Man, *don't* be aggravated!). But Tita has another, more unpredictable side: her fits of nervousness when she suddenly tries to break free. Sebastian, the hobby philosopher, thinks he has solved the "mystery of Tita." In his speech on the deforming nature of "order"—the new social order under Communism apparently being no different than the Prussian one she grew up under—he says about Tita: "you people all talk about degeneration. I'd say the veneer is cracking, and the individual underneath is finally reemerging." To Sebastian her delirium is a sign of sanity in a world that has gone insane.

A Party-loyal East German reviewer writing in the official newspaper was correct in his interpretation of de Bruyn's novel. "Frozen solid—nothing moves" was the title of his essay, in which he claimed that the novel purports to describe a world "that is supposed to be ours, but is his at best. . . . The author refuses to allow for development. Of course, development is futile when he is not out to probe and explore but to condemn." In the self-critical declaration issued by his publisher, de Bruyn—an acknowledged non-Marxist, non-Party member, and Catholic to boot—was apologetically described as writing from the "abstract viewpoint of a bourgeois-humanist 'moralist.'" The report explained that "[w]hen approving the manuscript at the publisher, a by no means unimportant consideration was that we can't give up trying to win over authors like de Bruyn so as to shield them from the even more intensified ideological influence of our class enemy." A scenario, of course, that would never play out.

New Glory, with its portrayal of total stagnation, in fact preceded a period of monumental change in Central Europe. Although no one imagined it at the time, the novel presciently foreshadowed the imminent demise of the GDR half a decade later. It is Thilde, with her dreams of "baking and travel," who expresses much of the discontent that would later bring down the communist regime in a growing wave of street protests. It may seem a banal point to make, but Germans, as a whole, are uncommonly fond of traveling (the pithy German expression *Fernweh*, an "aching for the faraway," captures this almost visceral desire quite nicely). One of the perennial bugbears of average East German citizens, therefore, was the restrictions they faced when it came to traveling. Only a select group of trusted individuals known as "travel cadre" could visit the West, for instance, and this with considerable red tape and security precautions (family members and loved ones generally had to stay behind). Viktor cynically tries to win the favor of Thilde's grandmother by exulting in the beauty of a bleak winter landscape in Brandenburg, saying "Who needs Switzerland!" when only he, a member of said "travel cadre," would ever know the difference. Then again, we never quite know where Viktor's good-naturedness ends and his dissembling begins.

At the end of the novel de Bruyn introduces the character of the pastor, who talks about "the placid surface and seething underground of a far-off age." He is intrigued by Tita's favorite song with its fateful refrain, "It cannot remain so forever, here under the changeable moon" (a German folk song with lyrics by August von Kotzebue). The pastor compares the society they live in with the Biedermeier period in German history,* the epitome of a stodgy, bourgeois, philistine society ("We sit here together so gaily, and love one another so much . . ."), an age characterized by retreat into the private sphere and a focus on domestic happiness—on "family values" if you will—at the expense of greater political freedom and individual development. It was a time of restoration, a reactionary period marked by political repression and censorship under Metternich's Carlsbad Decrees

---

*From the Vienna Congress of 1815 to the revolutions of 1848.

(issued after the murder of selfsame poet—and suspected Russian agent—August von Kotzebue by a radical student in 1819). It is interesting, and not entirely coincidental, that these thoughts are spoken by a clergyman. After all, the peaceful revolution that swept through East Germany and other communist states in 1989 began within the protective confines of the church, with an opposition movement that grew out of independent peace groups like one de Bruyn had briefly belonged to.

Grossman writes that "consciousness, in any situation, is always free to choose to face reality in a different, new way," and that "writing about reality is the simplest way to not be a victim." Viktor, in his passivity and conformism, is a victim, not a victor. Fear and habit stifle the sentence he desperately wants his father to hear: "I'm no longer a child you can lead by the nose!" Where Viktor fails, de Bruyn, the writer, succeeds—succeeds in expressing his "inner voice," succeeds, as the saying goes, in writing himself free.

Which is not to forget the novel's readers. In Eastern Bloc countries, critical literature played a crucial role as a moral force and alternative public sphere. In short, literature mattered in the GDR. Indeed, East German authorities had a respect for the written word that bordered on paranoia, tirelessly controlling every printed publication (a fact made all the more absurd considering that Western radio and television could be picked up, and were closely followed, throughout most of the GDR). But rather than laying claim to the "transformative power of literature" and turning de Bruyn into a dissident or prophet, we might do well to think of him as a chronicler. De Bruyn's literary testimony offers us an inside view of the state he lived and worked in for forty years, while reminding us, on a human level, that life behind the "Iron Curtain" was anything but monolithic.

Yet politics come and go. A work of art has enduring qualities. By grappling with the great human themes of love, freedom, death, and betrayal, *New Glory* achieves a timelessness which touches readers today, twenty-five years since first being published and twenty years after the fall of the Wall.

—*David Burnett*